BORDER BRAND

A

Mystery

RAOUL WHITFIELD

---

illustrations by Arthur Rodman Bowker

cover by Fred Craft

BLACK MASK

2024

Table of Contents

First Blood

THERE WAS A stiff wind blowing down from the north. It swept through the Mule Mountain pass, and I could imagine what it must be doing to Bisbee. Or perhaps that strange, mountain canyon town wasn't feeling it at all.

In any case, the windows in the hotel room were rattling. Dust blew up from the Douglas streets. The day had been hot and I was tired—dog tired. So tired that I was debating the extent of my thirst. Fifteen minutes' walk—and I'd be across the Line, in Agua Prieta, Mexico. I had a card to the Foreign Club. I knew Juan Garcia, who mixed drinks at the White House. I lighted a pill and rose from the edge of a hard bed. It was hard, even though it felt soft. I've been at the Border House when I wasn't dog tired—that's how I know about the beds.

The door opened, slowly. My eyes still burned from the sun glare, so I had the lights switched off. Yellow flashed into the room from a dim hall-light, but it didn't slant over my way. I stood with my back to the wall, and the fingers of my right hand gripped the Colt, inside the pocket of my suit. A figure slid inside; the door closed again. It was pretty neat work—hardly a click. Which meant just one thing. Oil had been used on the lock since I'd checked in and shaved. The Border House doesn't go in for well-oiled locks on its doors. As a matter of record—it doesn't go in for much of anything, with the exception of travelers' cash money.

I was wearing a dark suit—and so was the quiet caller. If my

head had been clearer than it was I *might* have played along with him. But it was too risky. Raising my left hand, I got a finger on the switch button. The room was flooded with light. Well, not exactly flooded. But there was plenty of nice, harsh, white light. No ritzy, soft lamps to give a fellow shadow.

The visitor faced me near the door. He was tall and pretty skinny. A bit round-shouldered, too. I noticed a few things right away, even though I had to blink a lot. The fellow held his hands by his sides. He had no weapon in them. And he was looking at my feet. Slowly his eyes traveled upward. He didn't swear, speak out. He seemed pretty cool. A lean, sun-browned face—gray, squinted eyes. There was something more in those eyes than a squint. They were a bit more than keen. And they were *not* piercing. His lips were thin; there was a faint smile playing around the corners of them. He was dressed so-so, in dark-colored material.

"Of course it's the wrong room," I stated slowly, grinning a bit. "Blowing a bit out, eh?"

The windows kept on rattling. The stranger's eyes went

down to my shoes again. He spoke in a husky tone. You'd have thought the fellow who possessed such a voice would be fat and fifty, or a tough pug, perhaps. This bird wasn't close to any of that.

"Bad flying weather, I'll bet," he observed slowly.

That gave me something to think about. It was my idea that I'd come into Douglas with a pretty bit of sky-sneaking. I figured that nobody in the town knew who I was or that the two-seater was out at the Carnival field. And I knew—now— that the husky-voiced gent was wise to several things. But I played along. Played the blue-eyed innocent.

"Do they fly aeroplanes down this way?" I asked, and had one hell of a time tacking the "aero" on the "plane."

The visitor let his eyes drop again. I was getting sore. Five hundred air miles in a new-engined ship isn't the biggest cinch in the world. And as I've stated before, I was tired.

"Maybe you don't like my feet?" I asked, with sarcasm. "And anyway, this happens to be my personal room. Suppose you just slide out the way you came in. I'll admit you do that well, and—"

"My name's Breed," this fellow interrupted quietly. "Ben Breed. I'm looking for a chap."

Well, he could have said a lot more—but in my case it would have been just extra work. I'd heard about Ben Breed. Most of the sky-riders who tin-can crates along the Border have heard of him. It made things a lot different. I took my fingers away from the Colt steel, and squatted on the bed again.

"Ten to one you'll get him," I stated cheerfully. "That is, if you're half so good as they say you are."

He didn't seem to hear me. "This chap," he said slowly, "is

a flyer. He's got a bad right leg, very small feet. He's also got ninety thousand American dollars and a cashier's bullet somewhere in his body. Your name's MacLeod. You flew in from the west, landed at the Carnival field. You pulled a sneak in here, and registered under the name of Jones. That's why I came in."

I nodded. "There's no bank cashier's lead in *my* frame," I stated, "and if I had ninety thousand I wouldn't head for Douglas."

This fellow Breed tossed me a pill, and lighted one for himself. He closed his eyes, inhaled.

"Business in town?" he asked in that husky voice of his.

I nodded, which forced him to open his eyes. After a few seconds of silence I gave him something to chew on.

"*Funny* business, too," I stated. "But nothing to do with a bank stick-up."

Breed's lips smiled. He nodded his head. There was a short silence. He broke it.

"All right—and when you spot me across the Line—just forget that I dropped in here. Sorry to bother you."

He turned toward the door. Then, suddenly, he stopped. I got off the bed. We both listened. Breed spoke first.

"Get a window up!" he snapped, and his tone gave me a jolt. No huskiness now. His words were clear, sharp. I got a window up. He was at my side. We both listened to the drone of a ship. It was high in the sky. And it sounded as if it were over Mexican sand and mesquite.

"There he goes," I muttered slowly. "With the ninety thousand."

Ben Breed shook his head. He was smiling.

"Missed it, Mac," he stated. "His plane has been down for

two hours— back in the Valley, near the south slope up to Bisbee. She's got a smashed prop—and no gas. And the killer's got a bad leg. In the nose-over, probably."

"Killer?" I stared at him with my eyes a bit wide. He chuckled.

"Surprised, eh?" he returned. And then—"Like hell you are, Mac! Well, see you later."

And with that he walked out of the room. I sat down on the edge of the bed again. How the devil did Breed know that I'd been five air-hours distant at the same time that the Wop had been five air-hours distant? And how did he know that I was wise to the fact that the Wop was a killer? Two men on the front steps of the Wheeler National.

I lighted the tip of one pill from the tip of another. I decided that Ben Breed *didn't* know that the Wop was the bank stick-up man. He'd guessed that I was going across the Line. He'd known who I was, and he'd get wise to my fake registration down in the cheap-smelling lobby of the Border House. And the Wop's ship had come down, nosed over. He knew that— and a few other things. He knew that I was playing innocent.

But here was the big kick—did he know that, in a money belt around my stomach, was the ninety-odd thousand that the Wop had got from the Arizona National? And the answer to that one was—he did not!

THE WHITE HOUSE was noisy. A Mex was trying to get American jazz out of a tinny piano that hadn't been tuned since Villa almost pulled a fast one and got to be somebody big. There were a few gringos sitting around in the big room. I gave Juan the high sign and went through some dirty curtains to one of the three back rooms. I was waiting for Juan to come along with my pet gin drink. The curtains rustled and Ben Breed eased into the room. He pulled out a chair from a yellow-green wall, and sat in close to me.

"Mac," he announced slowly and huskily, "you're a good guy. Prieta isn't the U.S.A. Not that I haven't walked some of the boys back from here. Who pulled the job, and who did the killing? Who's got the coin—and why in hell are you quitting the joy-hopping game to sit in with a bunch of crooks?"

He hadn't wasted any time getting to the point. I looked very puzzled, and then terribly blank. After a few seconds of that Juan came in with a *couple* of drinks. Which showed that Ben Breed had plenty of drag at the White House, too.

"What in hell's that?" I muttered, staring at the thin one's tall glass.

"Ginger ale," Breed returned. "Any objections?"

I yawned noisily. "It's no good, Bennie," I stated. "The more *I* drink the soberer I get."

Breed nodded. "If it affected me the same way," he replied, "I'd drink the same stuff you're drinking. What's the Wop doing these days, Mac?"

The gin fizz was in my throat, but I didn't choke. Juan went out through the curtains. I swore softly. I suddenly decided that Breed *did* know that the Wop had shot two guys out of their bank jobs and any other earthly jobs. I almost got worried. But I played along.

"What wop?" I asked casual-like. "The guy that makes that self-winding spaghetti over at Mexicali?"

Ben Breed tilted his chair back. "The wrong one, Mac," he stated cheerfully. "Natural mistake, though. I mean the one that tossed you the mail sack, up in Utah. Wheeler was the town, I believe. Right?"

I laughed out loud at that one, which shows that I should have been an actor. The jolts were coming fast and furious-like. Ben Breed wasn't even looking at me; he was sipping his ginger ale with his gray eyes half closed. Some Mex girl in the next room let out a sudden yell that pulled me up stiff in the chair. Breed set his glass down and yawned.

"Tough trip down, eh?" he asked slowly. "Even with a breeze on your two-seater's tail. Pretty bumpy, eh?"

I tried getting sore. "Listen here, Ben—lay off the funny stuff!" I muttered. "I *saw* a vaudeville show up at—"

I stopped. Ben Breed looked at me and grinned. He had a nice sort of smile; it wasn't cold or hard, not when he didn't want it to be. His gray eyes twinkled.

"Up around. Phoenix, I suppose. A couple of nights ago. Did the Wop laugh, too?"

I shrugged my shoulders. Breed leaned back in his chair and half closed his eyes again. I did some swift thinking. Here I was across the Line. Ninety grand next to my skin. The Wop was somewhere in the section. He'd stuck up the Wheeler National—and two gents had been killed. Ben Breed was working on the job, and I was to be the goat. That is, maybe I was. It all depended on how good or how rotten I performed.

One thing was certain. Breed had plenty of suspicion. And yet, he was doing a lot of talking. It sounded foolish; that is, it *might* have sounded foolish to a guy who didn't know Breed. There are two sorts of reputations a fellow gets along the Border. Ben Breed had the right kind. He was a man hunter. Rumor had it that he'd only missed one deal. And that deal was so tough that he'd spent three months in the El Paso Hospital. Two of "Mex" Arturo's men were permanently planted—and the Mex himself was off the Line.

Ben knew his stuff. He played the game from the inside. He worked sometimes fast—and sometimes slow. He was likely to turn up almost anywhere along the Border. He flew a single-seater with a rotary engine that had power. He had a telescopic camera mounted on the curved cowling, just in front of the cockpit. Maybe it was a camera—and maybe it was a machinegun. People didn't poke around his ship much. But the bad boys made a few guesses. I'd heard tales of Ben Breed along the Border for over a year, and this was the first time I'd run into him. Or he'd run into me, to be more accurate. And it wasn't exactly the right time for the thing to happen—not from my viewpoint.

He sat across the round-topped table from me, and sipped his ginger ale. The Mex girl in the big room had cut out yelling. Wind rattled the windows on this side of the Line, too. Breed spoke.

"You got a rotten deal at Wheeler, Mac," he stated. "I'll admit that. Let's see—two years ago, wasn't it? Nice war record you had, too. Don't suppose you remember me. Wore the two-bar stuff, and instructed you at Issoudun. Never forget a face. Funny, isn't it? Big help, though."

He smiled, lowered the glass of ginger ale to the table. I took a long swallow of the gin fizz. I was trying to play dumb, but every word this man Breed was getting rid of was registering. Scared? Well, I wouldn't say that. But I wasn't feeling a bit comfortable.

"Good pilot you were, Mac," he went on. "Got yourself a

Boche or two, unofficially, didn't you? A bank job, after the war—that must have seemed pretty slow. Did all right, though. Looked like you'd get to be cashier, eh? And then the Wop pulled a fast one—and grabbed himself fifty grand. And the directors sort of thought that a paying teller should have put up some kind of a scrap, eh? Particularly when he's been something of a war hero. And a few days later you cleared out—jumped Wheeler. Been coming around the Border off and on, ever since. Two years ago—this Wop knocked off that bank. And then early this morning he hits them again. For almost double the coin he grabbed before. Cracks up over near Bisbee—and you sky-ride into town with that crate of yours just a little later. Funny old world, isn't it, Mac?"

"Funny as hell," I agreed, and tried to keep my voice level. "All right, you got my record pat. But I've been joy-hopping them since the directors figured I should have made a move and filled myself full of lead. Maybe you know that, too."

Breed nodded. His gray eyes twinkled. He sipped some more ginger ale.

"Sure you have, Mac," he said more slowly and pleasantly. "Sure you have."

I didn't like the way he said it. Oh, it was all right on the surface. But he was getting me. With that smile, and the way he talked. He was smooth—just like the blade of a Mex dirk. And about as sharp. I got up from my chair, moved toward the small window that was rattling. The noise it made was getting on my nerves. I reached for a match to stick between the frame and—

The window went up. I caught a flash of something that might have been a dirty, bare arm. The blade was silver in the light. My whole body stiffened—I jerked my head to one side. It missed my throat by a couple of inches. There was a pop-cough from behind me. I let myself drop to the floor. The knife clattered against the yellow-green wall opposite the small window. A breeze kicked up dust from the rough board floor.

I jerked around, looking for Breed. He was sitting in his chair, leaning forward. His thin lips were pressed tightly together. But he was smiling. His right hand held the gun and rested, at the same time, on the table surface. The gun was leveled at the open window. It was one of those small-calibred foreign affairs that'll take a silencer on the muzzle. I could see the round attachment.

"Stick up a hand—shut the window!" His voice was sharp again, no huskiness. "He's gone—and my lead didn't even give him breeze. Then come on back and lie to me some more."

I stuck up a hand and shut the window. Ben Breed was right, of course. There wasn't any use in getting out of the White House and pulling a fool search. We'd just be a couple of targets for anything that somebody wanted to send our way. I moved back toward the chair I'd just vacated.

Breed took a clean handkerchief out of his pocket and picked up the knife with it. He set it on the table, slipped his automatic back into a pocket. I said, as calmly as I could:

"Wasn't lying to you, Bennie."

He reached for his ginger ale. He nodded. The wind rattled the frame again.

"Where's the ninety grand, Mac?" he asked quietly. "Got it on you?"

I tossed off the rest of my drink. It was pretty hot inside the room. I commenced to feel sick. It didn't seem to me as if my heart was pumping just right. It was making a lot of noise. Ben

Breed was smiling at me. I tried to get out of the chair—and almost did. Everything was getting hazy, misty. Breed seemed to be a long way off. He said something and I didn't get half of it. A lot of thick words. My hands felt as if they had thick gloves fastened on them.

"The—drink—drugged it on—"

My tongue was all twisted up. I tried to curse Juan, to curse Ben Breed. And then my head pitched down on the table—and everything was black and still.

I CAME OUT of it with a headache and a weak feeling all over. There was sunlight in the room and the room was the one I'd taken at the Border House. I sat up on the edge of the bed—and groaned. I was almost stripped of my clothing, which was thrown over a chair nearby. The ninety grand!

It was gone. The money belt was gone. I got off the bed, headed for the little basin. Cold water on my face and body—and I felt a bit better. Two aspirin. My wrist watch was on the chair—it showed that noon was approaching. I opened the two windows in the room wide. The wind had died down; it was almost hot outside. I dressed slowly.

Well, it was a cinch. And then again, it wasn't a cinch. Ben Breed had drugged my drink. He was in the clear; he'd got the ninety grand from alongside of my skin. The last I could remember of him was that smile—and the way he leaned back in his chair. But someone had brought me back across the Line, got me to this room. Who? Breed? And if so, why?

I moved toward the door. It was locked. I lifted a foot, and then changed my mind. On the faded carpet near the door was a key. And near the key was a folded piece of paper. I picked up the paper, Unfolded it. There was red smeared on the inside. Blood. It almost obliterated some of the scrawled words. The pencil hadn't had much of a point, anyway. I read in a low voice.

"Hell broke loose across the Line. Game's big. Stick inside until I come in—got you back and tossed the key through transom, after locking you in. Got a knife through the wrist—for the Wop and his outfit—first blood."

That was all. I read the scrawled words several times. Then I picked up the key and stuck it in the lock. Ben Breed had got me back, and he'd taken a dirk prick. He was coming over to see me. The Wop had popped up across the Line, and things had been hot—*after* I'd been drugged. And I was to stick inside and wait for Breed to show.

Like hell I was! There were too many funny things. In the first place, I was taking Breed's word for the fact that he was Ben Breed. He did fit in with the general description I'd had of him, but that wasn't any real proof. The big thing was that I'd been drugged and the ninety grand was gone. Supposing someone had wanted to pull the job smooth-like. Someone who had a drag with Juan. I'd look pretty sitting inside a room, and waiting—while the guy who'd pulled the job ducked with the coin. A lot of money—ninety grand was. A lot.

I twisted the key in the lock. All right. I'd been brought back. I was alive. The door had been locked, but the key had been tossed inside. A good gag. But I wasn't that easy. The fellow who had framed me could risk that little stunt—giving me a key. I'd had a long sleep. He might have figured that he could gain more time—with his bluff.

Stick inside? Wait? Nothing like that. I shoved the door open, stiffened. Before me stood Ben Breed. He looked tired.

There were white bandages on his left wrist. But he was smiling that tight-lipped smile of his. I took a step back and to one side. Ben came in. I shut the door and locked it. He dropped into the nearest chair.

"Feel better, Mac?" he asked in his husky voice. "Did you get your gun?"

"Yes and no," I returned grimly.

"Under the pillow," he said slowly. "Easy how you handle it—plenty of lead inside."

I didn't even look at the pillow. Instead, I sat down on the edge of the bed.

"Look here, Breed—" I muttered—"if you *are* Breed—which I'm not sure about. Come through with the details!"

He grinned. "Someone stuffed your liquor full of sleep," he stated. "I figured, at the start, that you were acting up. Then you flopped—and hell popped loose. The lights went out. A bunch of greasers filled the room. I couldn't see 'em—but I could smell 'em. They tossed a few knives, and one of them stood up against a wall and used an automatic. He neglected to keep moving, and I got him after the second flash. I knew where you were, so I squeezed lead around a lot—and kept moving until a knife got me in the wrist. Then I squatted. A Mex slammed me on the head with something. When I came up for air the room was filled with border inspectors. You were present. There was one dead Mex. He wasn't the Wop. I knew one of the inspectors—Pedro Cordoza. He said his bunch were just going off duty at the Line. They heard the shooting. Thought it was the usual drunken brawl. When they came in— the others went out. Five or six of 'em. They got one of them—a Mex who gave his name as Garcia Avenosio. I got a flivver and brought you up here. Then I headed for a doc, got my wrist fixed up. After that I went to bed."

I looked Ben Breed right in his gray, cheerful eyes.

"What do you suppose it was all about?" I asked simply.

Ben shook his head, shrugged his shoulders. He looked his age this morning—around forty, I'd have said. His hair was dark, sort of mussed up. But he didn't look stupid. And he didn't talk that way.

"Maybe they thought we had some coin on us," he said slowly.

"Sure, that's it!" I came back, "That's why Juan drugged my gin. Sure!"

Breed was frowning. "Well, he won't drug it any more," he stated. "Someone pushed a knife through his back—and he went to Mexican heaven before *you* started to sleep."

I swore softly, got up off the bed. Juan finished off. But he'd brought the drinks in. My eyes narrowed on Breed's. The thing was pretty big. There was just one way of playing it. Clean. But first I'd make sure of one thing.

"I'd like to gab some, Breed," I said slowly. "First, I'd like to know that you're right to gab with. If you're Ben Breed—I'll play straight. Anything that might convince me?"

He smiled. "Not a damn thing!" he snapped coldly. "I don't carry papers around."

I nodded. "Yeah, I've heard that one, too," I returned. "And if you *weren't* Breed, and had any brains, that's what you'd say. All right—I don't talk."

He chuckled. "Let me do it for you, Mac," he said slowly. "I'll start from the place where the Wop ran out of gas and headed for the mesquite and sand on the Valley south of Mule Mountain. The place you headed for in that nice, new-engined Waco of yours—at about the same time. Good place to start?"

I stopped walking around and making my head feel worse. Besides, Breed was banging them in pretty accurate like. I sat down on the bed again. He went right on talking.

"You weren't looking for the Wop. But here was a strange ship, dead-propping it for a landing place. So you kicked up sand close by. Flores had just got clear of the ship and was wandering around in a daze—when you came up on him. You recognized each other at the same time—and you both pulled rods. He missed you—and your lead was low, but you hit him in the right leg. He'd already been plugged in the left shoulder, hours before. That's why he missed you. When you got him in the leg he collapsed. You looked him over—and grabbed the ninety grand. Then you saw a single-seater come down out of the clouds. You stuck around until it was sure that the single-seater pilot was coming down to have a look at a nosed-up ship and another ship. Then you took the coin, climbed back into your Waco—and headed for Douglas. You know the rest."

I stared at the man who sat with his chair tilted against the dirty wall of the Border House room. He closed his eyes again. I got up, and then sat down. I reached under the pillow on which my head had rested, and found my Colt. It was all loaded. I tossed it back on the pillow.

"Ben," I said slowly. "You win the ninety grand. You've got me right from two years back. From the war, maybe. And you're Breed, all right. That's that. You bluffed me plenty, right in here last night. And all the time you weren't looking for the Wop at all. What was the game?"

Ben Breed smiled that pleasant smile of his. Then, sort of sudden-like, it got hard.

"Had a hunch you were sitting in with the greaser, Mac. You see, I got to Flores just after you lifted your crate off the sand. When he came out of it I told him all about the wire we'd got, all along the Border. I told him he was a damned fool to go and stick up the bank again. He *almost* came through with me—and then he didn't feel that money belt next to his brown skin. So he tried a bluff. I did some quick thinking. Johnny Green came along in a flivver—he'd spotted the ships diving and taking off from the sand. I told him to take Flores to the Douglas hospital. Then I hit the air, and picked up your ship at the Carnival field. After that I came into town. Johnny Green was *in* the hospital. The Wop wasn't. He'd slammed Johnny over the head with the flivver crank, and got clear. I traced you to this room. What about the ninety grand, Mac?"

I stared at him. Then my eyes narrowed. The game was still wide open. There were a lot of things I didn't know. And *maybe* there was something Ben Breed didn't know.

"What about it?" I asked slowly.

He sat up straight in the chair. His eyes bored into mine. There was no smile on his face. He looked hard. He was hard—right now.

"You got it?" he snapped.

I shook my head. *"You've* got it!" I snapped back. "Come out in the open. Come out all the way. I'll play with you, Ben."

He leaned toward me. His voice was cold like ice. And sharp.

"You *had* it—across the Line, Mac?"

I hesitated, then nodded. He swore fiercely. His lips were pressed together in a thin line.

"Mac—" he said quietly—"what I wrote in that note is straight. First blood—for Antonio Flores. The Wop had that coin. He stuck up the Wheeler bank. The wires burned up with that news. Guess you got it, too. Then you spotted his ship—and grabbed the ninety. I was hot after you, but I didn't think you'd take the coin across the Line with you. Damned if I did."

I looked him in the eyes. "Until you slipped inside this room I didn't figure on taking it with me, Ben," I returned. "But that made things different."

He got to his feet from the chair. His voice had lost a lot of the huskiness. And his shoulders weren't so stooped. He stood straight, looking down at me. His words came out hard.

"What were you going to do with that coin, Mac?" he snapped.

I gave it to him straight. "Take it back to Wheeler—throw it in the faces of the bunch that fired me!" I snapped. "Believe that one?"

Ben Breed nodded. "It's on the level," he said slowly. "I talked to you like a man talks to a crook—last night. But I know your record, MacLeod. It's on the up. You knew the Wop doesn't work alone. You knew there'd be trouble getting that coin back. And you wanted to play it your way. But the Wop's Border-bred. He's half Mex, half Italian. He can toss a knife—I guess you know that. He had us right—across the Line."

I groaned. "Ninety grand—and he got it on the right side of the Line—for him. He can go to lots of places in Mexico—and be safe. *First* blood, you say? And then some, Ben? They got two guys back in Utah. They got Juan. They almost got us. And they got the coin. It's what I call—"

"Easy!" Ben Breed was smiling again. "The coin's on the Mex side, Mac—but they haven't *got* it!"

I stiffened. I got the idea, all of a sudden, that Breed was handling me again. Playing with me. He hadn't come through, after all. He was still listening to me answer questions—and he knew the answers before he asked them.

"Don't hit the ceiling, Mac!" His voice was low, steady. "When the lights went out I ripped into your clothes—got that belt. Got the knife in my wrist doing that. Had a hunch you *might* pack the coin with you. Wasn't sure until I got my fingers on it. All in big bills, and packed smooth-like. Things were getting tough—it looked like one I wasn't going to get out of—they were swarming inside that black room. I got over against the wall, back of where I'd been sitting. There was an old phonograph there, one with a horn on it. A curved horn. I—"Ben Breed lowered his voice—"felt inside the horn and—"

The knob on the door moved. It made a clicking noise. Ben Breed jerked his head. I reached toward the pillow and grabbed my Colt. The transom above the door was half opened.

Ben stepped up close to the door. The knob had stopped moving. The white bandages on his left wrist showed as he snapped the key, jerked the door suddenly outward. It swung wide. Breed dropped to his knees. His automatic was held low. He was like a cat in his movements. And nerve—he had it. I lay flat on the bed, my Colt steadied for a sure squeeze.

Breed was out in the corridor now. His body vanished from sight. I lay motionless. Seconds passed. My eyes were on the faded corridor carpet. I started to call out his name, then changed my mind. I'd say about ten seconds passed. Then I slipped from the bed. I reached the door. A knife could do quiet work. I've heard of guys getting a fellow, and then catching him in their arms. No fall sound, no crashing down.

I stuck my head outside, with my eyes taking in everything.

And I saw all there was to see. It wasn't much. There was no sight of Ben Breed. No sound in the corridor. I stood there, gun in hand. I thought back, and I thought fast. Ben Breed had come in. He'd talked. I'd talked. I didn't remember any phonograph or horn in the room at the White House. I'd told Ben several things that he'd wanted to know. A door knob had moved—and he'd ducked.

A plant? Someone outside, and listening in? A signal for Ben Breed? But why?

I swore softly. The corridor made a sharp turn to the right, twenty feet from my doorway. Go down—and make the turn? A blank wall, ten feet the other direction. Just one way to go. Yeah, but hadn't Breed known that? Did he figure I was going to chase out that way? He had a silencer on his gun.

That was no good. He'd had plenty of chance to finish me off, inside the room, and after he'd got information he *might* have wanted. My head wasn't clear enough to sit in this way. It was too tough. The ninety grand was gone. I turned back into the room. Then I froze, just inside the door. I started to raise my Colt—and stopped that right away. Standing near the basin, at one side of the bed, was a short, thick-set individual. He had a nasty-looking rod in his right hand; the muzzle of it was leveled right at my stomach. His face was fat and brown. Greasy. There was a twisted smile on his lips—a short scar ran downward from his lower lip, over his chin.

I stood still, and tried to get my breath. After a few seconds I got it. My voice wasn't very loud, and it certainly wasn't steady. But I got out the words. Not that they meant much.

"Hello, Flores!"

The smile vanished. He started to curse. He mixed Mex with

English, and talked through tight-pressed lips. He shifted his gun a bit, raised it. Then he called me one name that he'd been saving up for the finish. I felt it coming. He squeezed the trigger.

THE CRASH OF the gun in that small room came simultaneously with the flash of an arm. The arm shot out from the closet in which I'd placed my one bag. It battered to one side the hand of the Wop's—the one that held the gun. Then, as the bullet cracked along the plaster of the wall, a clenched fist caught the Wop just under the right ear. Flores pitched forward.

I raised my gun a bit—and the voice of Ben Breed sounded, sharply.

"Don't shoot, Mac! Grab his gun!" The Wop was trying to pull himself to his knees. I put a foot on the wrist I wanted to pin down, and jerked the gun loose. Ben Breed fished into his pocket and snapped out a pair of steel cuffs. They were thin— and they looked strong. The Wop was on his knees. He was weak, stunned. I reflected that Ben's wallop was in his left. He'd used the right to batter a bullet away from my body.

Ben stepped in close, got the Wop's arms behind his back, got his wrists together. The cuff-steel clicked. He gave the Wop a shove into one of the two chairs in the room. Then he grinned at me.

"Almost lost him, Mac," he stated. "That closet of yours leads out to the corridor. Flores was set for a kill. He fooled with that knob—then jumped for the closet. Slipped in and shut the corridor door. I got in just about right, eh?"

I nodded. The Wop was staring at Ben Breed. His face

was sullen; his little rat-eyes gleamed. He started to speak, thickly—and then stopped. I swore softly.

"This is a hell of a hotel!" I muttered. "Closet doors opened to the outside—"

"A chap by the name of Benecio runs it, under cover for a red-headed Irishman by the name of Burke," Breed stated grimly. "Benecio's Mex."

My eyes went to the Wop. The scar on his chin stood out like Mule Mountain on a clear day. Ben Breed looked at me.

"What do they do in Utah, Mac?" he asked grimly. "Burn electricity inside of 'em—or break their necks on the gallows?"

I shook my head. "You got me, Ben," I returned. "But if you mean the Wop, here—they'll lynch him as soon as he crosses the Line. Maybe before."

The Wop twisted in the chair, swore savagely. Then, suddenly, he quieted down.

"Lynch me?" he muttered thickly. "What for?"

I grinned. "Breaking and entering, taking and leaving—shooting and killing," I replied grimly. "Not just once, at that."

Flores sneered. "Where do *you* get off, you cheap quitter?" he muttered. "And where'd you plant the coin?"

I kept right on grinning. "Spent it, Wop," I stated. "Beer and gin—and the beer wasn't worth it. Too green."

Ben Breed spoke. "Watch him, Mac," he stated. "I'll go down to the desk and call the chief of police. I don't *think* he's the Wop's brother."

Breed went out. I sat down on the edge of the bed and looked at the Wop. He was a dirty little killer, and he'd caused me plenty of trouble. I tried to figure his game in trying for a noisy kill—and gave it up. I figured he was just sore at me for grabbing the money belt, back beside his wrecked ship. Then I thought of the moving knob, and remembered what we'd been talking about. The Wop knew something. Breed would be a damned fool if he turned the killer over to the police. If Flores got word out—

"Ten grand—if you ease me out of this room!"

The Wop spoke hoarsely. His words broke up my thoughts. I shook my head.

"And eighty thousand for you?" I snapped. "Do I look sick?"

Flores scowled at me. He twisted in the chair, as I inspected his gun. There were voices down the corridor, raised, excited. I guessed that Ben Breed was explaining about the shot, and trying to keep the others away from the room. Flores spoke again.

"Twenty-five grand—and I'll call the boys off, take you off the spot!" he offered.

I swore at him. "Where's the coin?" I snapped. "On paper?"

The Wop narrowed his eyes. "You can put a gun on me—keep the cuffs on until a frail hands it over. It'll take a ten-minute walk. The coin's right."

I grinned. "I got over being *that* dumb—two years ago," I stated. "I can walk you into Mexico, all right. And the frail you steer me to can get your pals to come in and see that my gun doesn't do any harm to your skin. Nothing doing, Wop."

Flores grinned. It was a nasty grin. He shrugged his wide shoulders.

"Take your choice," he said slowly. "It's me or Ganlin. He's slippin' out on you now, and that's jake stuff."

I sat up pretty straight on the edge of the bed. Ganlin— "Cards" Ganlin! So named because he'd started his game with the pasteboards and a poker face. A sweet bluffer, and a keen brain. One of the cleverest crooks on the Border. I'd seen him once, down Mexican Imperial Valley, down near Black Butte. It came back slowly. Tall, he'd been. Round shouldered and sort of thin. I remembered the way he'd dealt cards—left-handed. And the gent who called himself Ben Breed had slapped the Wop down with a left, I remembered a few other things—among them that I hadn't seen any phonograph in the little White House room.

The Wop's dark eyes were on mine. He seemed to guess what I was thinking. There was only one way to play it—now. I yawned noisily.

"Try another line, Wop," I suggested. "That last one wasn't funny enough."

I got a surprise. The Wop didn't get sore. He just shrugged his shoulders again.

"You're in tight," he said slowly. "They'll ride you to hell if you let Cards get away with the coin."

I kept smiling. The Wop remained silent. Five minutes passed. Ten. Fifteen. The Wop spoke. His voice was thick.

"He's in the clear—with the stuff you grabbed from me. If they get me—I'll see that you get the limit. An' Cards won't get so far that the boys don't find him."

Cards Ganlin! I thought of the ninety grand next to my skin, over at the White House. I thought of the drugged fizz. That was about the way Ganlin would sit in on the deal. He'd know there was the Wop to lick, too. So he'd play me against the Wop. I got up from the bed, walked toward the window that faced to the north. I could see Mule Mountain in the distance, across the Valley. There was a cracked mirror hanging on the wall between the basin and the window. The Wop was grinning. I didn't like it. Did Flores run the police of the town? Was he sure of getting out of the cuffs? Or was he just bluffing?

I half turned—and then it sounded. A roar. Blocks away, and yet not so many blocks away, at that. The roar died. Over the tops of several two-story, frame buildings to the north of the hotel, rose a cloud of smoke and dust. A staccato crackling beat in on the silence. Down in the narrow street I could see people running, running toward the cloud, of smoke and dust. The steam-rivet clatter ceased. Then it started again. A police whistle shrilled. There was another roar—no smoke or dust this time. I glanced in the mirror. The Wop was stiff in the chair.

"Something's up!" I muttered grimly. "If Breed was—"

The Wop chuckled. "Maybe it's the Douglas National," he suggested. "Sounded in that direction."

My eyes narrowed on Flores' little slitted ones. A police whistle was shrilling again; the machine-gun had stopped beating out its staccato sound. The street below seemed empty. A black, open car purred past the hotel, headed for the Border and Agua Prieta.

I swore softly. Something big was on, up toward the center of town, and I was stuck up in a hotel room, wet-nursing a handcuffed killer. And the Wop didn't seem much disturbed about what was happening. I got that, clearly. It seemed to me that he sort of *expected* something to happen.

I made a quick decision, moved away from the window toward him. I was playing in the dark—I'd let the Wop take the same sort of dose. He had almost enough on me for a frame-up. I'd have a sweet time going back to Wheeler and telling the police and the bank officials that I'd grabbed ninety

grand from him—just to take back and throw in their faces—
and then I'd lost the coin. Sweet, that would be.

"Get up out of that chair!" I snapped. "Walk—out and
downstairs. Stick close to me. If you make a break I'll let loose
more lead than you ever felt before. Come on!"

He pulled himself out of the chair. I was right back of him,
with my Colt inside a loose pocket of my jacket. We went
down the ancient stairs, into the narrow lobby. The clerk wasn't
around. No one was around. We headed for the street. The Wop
jerked his head. He was limping a little.

"Listen!" he muttered. "You can't ride me for this deal. I got
to see somebody."

I jammed the Colt up close to his back.

"Keep moving!" I snapped, "or you won't any more!"

Flores walked out into the street. A figure was running
toward us. It was the hotel clerk. He almost banged into the
Wop. I grabbed him by the arm. He was white-faced.

"What's doing?" I snapped.

"The bank!" he panted. "They—blew her up. Got machine-
guns. A lot of people killed—I got to telephone!"

I let him go, but the Wop got in his way.

"You crook!" he shouted. "Look at me—cuffed up! You got
me framed. I've been up there for fifteen minutes, with this
guy watching me. You did it!"

The clerk stared at the Wop. I shoved Flores out of the way.

"Buzz the wires!" I snapped. "He's talking rot!"

The clerk was staring at the steel cuffs. His lips moved. He
was pretty excited.

"I didn't frame you!" he muttered. "I didn't even know—"

"Get a phone!" I cut in. "The Wop's trying to alibi himself, that's all. I grabbed him just now, a block away. He was duck-ing away from the bank."

Flores jerked his body around. His face was white with rage. I laughed at him. He started to curse as the hotel clerk went inside on a run.

A second car came around a corner, headed down the street toward the Border. I got behind Flores. There were two men in the rear seat of the car—one of them had a rifle. The rear left tire was flat—and the machine was running on the rim. I took a shot at the driver. The gent with the rifle swung it out, spotting Flores. He didn't fire. The car went banging and skid-ding down the street. I shoved the muzzle of my Colt through the hole the bullet had made in the khaki cloth of the jacket.

"Toward the bank!" I snapped. "And walk fast!"

Flores walked. People were coming out on the streets again. A fire truck sirened into sight. We were a block from the bank. I could see some smoke ahead, rising over the roof of an adobe building. The Wop was muttering to himself. We turned a corner. The bank was a block ahead, across the street. There wasn't much of a crowd in sight. I counted four figures lying in the yellow dust of the street. The front of the bank was pretty badly wrecked. Smoke rose from the ruins. A short, thick-set man came walking toward us, his lips moving—no words coming from between them. He held both hands just under his heart, and as he got about ten feet away he collapsed with a little, hissing sound. I stopped Flores, took a look. The short gent was dead.

A gun cracked from a roof across the street. I thought my ears picked up the whine of the lead. The Wop groaned, sagged forward, pitched down heavily. He lay on his face. There was a doorway behind me. I got inside a narrow hall. Things weren't finished yet. But I guessed that the Wop was. He looked that way.

I heard something else. A ship's engine droning in the distance. It had a thin sound. A small plane—rotary-engined. I stiffened a bit. My eyes went to the sky.

The Wop rolled over suddenly. He tried to move his hands from behind his back. My eyes came away from the sky. Flores was still alive. There was red over the lower part of his face. It hid the scar. He muttered something. I went out from the doorway, kneeled down beside him. He muttered thickly.

"Cards Ganlin—running the bank—job! Get-away in—plane. I'm—done—he double-crossed me an'—"

He stopped muttering, closed his eyes. I straightened. A ship came into sight. She was flying low, heading for Mexico. She roared over the street—then banked sharply. I swore. She was the ship I'd seen come down out of the clouds, after I'd landed my two-seater beside the nosed-up plane landed by the Wop. Breed's plane—or Cards Ganlin's? Which?

I heard a sound back of me. Instinctively I twisted around, swung up to my feet. There was the flash of steel—and then—the Wop's voice!

"No—lay off that—"

I tried to get my gun up. The Wop kicked out savagely with both feet. I went down, knocked off balance. Something struck me heavily in the back of the head. For the second time, within twenty-four hours, everything went black.

WHEN I CAME out of it I was lying in the lobby of the Border House. There were two or three humans crowded around me. I could feel one of them sopping my head with something cold and wet. They helped me to my feet, and I looked around. Someone said something about a doctor, and someone else said that they were all busy with guys that were really hurt. No one laughed. I was helped to a chair, and sat down. Someone wanted to know what had happened. I said that there was a lot of excitement—and I'd been slammed down by some bird from behind. A couple of fellows left me and headed for the street. A tall, thin bird stuck around and told me I hadn't been hurt much—just a blackjack wallop on the head. I nodded, and he disappeared to get me a glass of water.

The hotel clerk came over and started asking a lot of questions about the Wop. I was trying to get things straight by thinking back, and between the drugged drink and my wallop on the head that wasn't easy. The clerk stopped asking questions and told me what had happened.

The Douglas National had been blown up—or part of it had, anyway. The crooks had got away with almost a hundred thousand. There had been a half dozen of them, maybe more. They'd had machine-guns planted in several places, and one gent had stood in the entrance of a store near the bank and picked off police with an automatic rifle. There were four citizens dead—and two police. Not one of the crooks had been found. That was the first stuff that had got out.

The thin bird came back with the water. The clerk was saying that the Wop wasn't in on the deal, because hadn't he seen him hand-cuffed, and with me? And what was it all about? I played sick. I felt that way. The telephone rang at the desk, and the clerk went over to answer it. I handed the glass back to the tall, thin individual. He was tough-looking, and I didn't like the way he grinned. He dropped the glass on the floor, and kicked the pieces under my chair.

Then he slid up an automatic from a hip pocket, held it at his side, concealed from the clerk at the desk. He spoke.

"You an' me are takin' a walk. Just like you an' the Wop took one—only this ends different. Get on your feet—an' outside! Turn right—and head for the Line. We're goin' over to the White House for a drink."

I looked at his eyes and decided that he was right. I knew a lot of things—and the Wop didn't like to have guys walking around who knew things. It was just too bad that I hadn't let Flores and his ninety grand strictly alone. I thought of Ben Breed, or the guy who called himself Ben Breed—and swore grimly. Someone had got the double-cross. Maybe one or two of us.

It was shaky walking until I hit the street. Then the air seemed to help a little. I felt the top of my head. It was cut and swollen. The tall bird walked back of me, and whistled. I wondered how he figured we'd get across the Line. The American inspectors would have plenty of questions to ask. I wondered how the car with the flat tire, and the guy with the rifle had got across. I decided that it hadn't, and that its driver hadn't made the attempt. And I figured that maybe we weren't headed that way—not all the way.

We'd made about five squares toward Agua Prieta when a black car came around a corner and pulled up at the side of the road which the street had become. There were shacks all around, but no one seemed to be in sight. All down at the bank, I figured. The car stopped, and the gent behind me, lighting a pill, told me to climb inside. From the way he acted care-less, I knew there were guns on me from inside the car, which was closed and had dirty windows. A door opened—I got in. Someone grabbed me and pulled me down. The door slammed. I looked to my right. The Wop was grinning nastily. He was cleaning his fingernails with a match.

"Hello!" he greeted. "Feel like talking? We're goin' to a place for that reason."

I sat back in the seat. Then I looked to my left. I got a shock. Sitting back in the seat with his eyes closed, and looking a lot like he was sleeping, was Ben Breed! Or maybe Cards Ganlin. Anyway, one of the two.

The car was in motion. It turned a corner, to the left. *Away* from the Border. My head was aching badly; I tried to smooth my forehead skin out by rubbing. The Wop noticed me doing it.

"That'll be all right," he stated grimly. "You won't feel it in an hour or so."

I was perfectly willing to believe that one. And I knew what sort of talking he wanted me to do. It was up to the gent who'd called himself Ben Breed to do the talking. I just didn't know—not about the ninety grand.

The car was bouncing over a rough road now. It kept it up for about ten minutes. There was a guy beside the driver who kept jerking his head behind. The fellow who had brought me the drink and then escorted me from the hotel—he was riding beside the driver. He sat facing the rear seat, and he held his automatic in sight. The car slowed down, stopped.

The Wop spoke. "All out—change cars for hell!"

We got out—all but the fellow I was about ready to think was Cards Ganlin. The Wop jerked him out. He had a grim smile on his face. We were on a narrow road. There were hills all around, and plenty of mesquite. We weren't so far from the Border. The driver said something to the Wop that I didn't catch. The long, thin individual told me to walk in a certain direction. I did, waiting to take a bullet in my back. But it didn't come. I heard the car get under way. The Wop called to me, and I halted, turned. He waved a gun toward the other prisoner.

"Move up to your pal, Ben!" he muttered.

I waited. The Wop had called the man he had once before called Cards Ganlin—only this time he had called him Ben. It looked like the beginning of the finish—where the truth wouldn't hurt. We stood side by side, facing the Wop. Brains— that guy had. I thought of the bullet that had been fired from somewhere, back in town. Flores had used that sweetly. A fake fall, a split lip for some red stuff—and then he'd talked some lies—and kicked me off my balance even as a pal had battered me down from behind. But he was calling Breed by his right name now. Why had he tried to bluff me, back in town?

Well, I'd know. The Wop would tell. That was his type. He'd talk—and then we'd go out. The game was big.

Flores stood about ten feet in front of us, his short legs spread apart. His lower lip was badly swollen. His scar stood out plainly. He grinned.

"Over the hill back of you law-boys is a level stretch of sand," he stated slowly. "Two ships on it. One's a two-seater. It belonged to another guy until about ten minutes ago. Then he tried a double-cross, and went to a place where they don't count, I'm making you guys a present of it. The other belongs to Bennie Breed, man-hunter." The Wop chuckled hoarsely. "I'm handling that baby. Bennie's just given me some information.

Things are pretty hot and getting hotter. A couple of nice, clean boys are heading for Agua Prieta, to look at a phonograph in the White House. You two can take off in the two-seater. Breed rides in rear cockpit. I'll fly the single-seater. We'll get five thousand—and circle over Agua Prieta. I'm looking for a ground-strip signal. All right—let's stroll."

"I'm not a law-boy, Wop," I said slowly. "You're not loading me with lead for *that*."

Flores grunted. "You play in with one," he stated. "What do you mean—loading you with lead? Ain't I letting you in the clear?"

Ben Breed spoke. His voice was husky; his eyes were on mine.

"Sure he's letting us free, Mac—I gave him the dope on the ninety grand. Had to—one of his gang got a rod on me when I went down to phone. Kept me out of sight until they pulled this Douglas job. And if my single-seater's here—they used it."

The Wop grinned. "Wise as hell!" he stated. "Where you guys are going it'll be a great help to be clever. I'll give it to you straight. Cards Ganlin used your single-seater, Breed—to get the money down out here, after the transfer. Only he held out on Red—so we spotted him out. All right—move!"

We moved—the Wop behind us. The two ships came into sight, in a sort of valley between the hills. No one was around. There were clumps of mesquite on the take-off stretch, but not enough of them to nose over a plane. The two-seater I'd never seen before. But that was clear. Cards Ganlin had moved about in a two-seater. He'd tried to play rough with Flores, and he didn't count. But the same thing went for Breed and myself. The Wop wasn't talking—not unless he knew that we would cease to count in a hurry.

Breed spoke in a low tone. "He'll get us—in the air!"

I stared at the gray-eyed one. He was smiling. The Wop spoke.

"Climb in—both of you. Rev her up—take off. Get five thousand—over Prieta. If you see a white sheet out, back of the White House—head westward. And *keep* flying Westward. If no white sheet shows, and the boys haven't got the coin where Bennie said it would be—just sit tight and take the fall. Get going!"

I faced the Wop. "You're crashing us—one way or the other," I stated. "Know why I wanted the ninety grand, Flores?"

He grinned. "Sure—for charity!" he snapped. "Climb in that ship before I change my mind and spill—"

Ben Breed gripped me by the arm. I got a foot on the wing-step. My head was aching as I slipped down into the front cockpit. Breed climbed into the one behind. I snapped the self-starter. There was a roar from behind. The single-seater's engine was revving up already. I jerked my head. Breed's face was sober. He spoke grimly.

"Get her off—and up, Mac!" he ordered. "He's got my Browning trained on us."

I thought of the telescopic camera that wasn't a camera—but a Browning. The self-starter switch snapped—the two-seater's engine roared. I cut it down. A voice drifted to us, from behind.

"Don't use those 'chutes—law boys!" It was mocking in tone. Ben Breed stuck his head close to mine.

"No 'chutes—take her off!" he muttered above the beat of the engine.

I advanced the throttle. The plane rolled forward. Mesquite tugged at the left wheel—but she got past. We gained speed. Then I lifted her, banked almost off the sand, cleared the crest of the slope. I jerked my head. The single-seater was coming up behind us and to the right. Just out of the prop wash. I could see the barrel of the Browning. We roared toward the air above Agua Prieta.

I could see it from the Wop's side. A clean kill, in the sky. We'd crash on the Mexican side—that would make things tougher for a trace. The two-seater would burn, ten to one. The Wop was fairly safe in Breed's single-seater. He had the loot from the Douglas job, pulled off by the man he'd tried to make me believe Breed had been—Cards Ganlin. He could fly clear of Douglas and Agua Prieta—and the chase.

Ben Breed's head was close to mine. His voice sounded in my ears as he leaned across the curved surface of the fuselage, separating the two cockpits.

"No ninety grand—at White House! His men won't find— the coin! He's sky-spotting us! Sorry—Mac—wasn't sure of you, first!"

I jerked my head, tried to grin. The ship had two thousand, was over Agua Prieta. I stared down over the side. There was no sign of a white ground-strip. I could see the roof of the White House. Twisting my head again, I saw the single-seater. The Wop had her above us now. I banked wildly, feeling out the plane. She handled sluggishly, but tilted a wing to the sky, a wing to the earth. I climbed her in the bank. Up above us the single-seater was climbing. Ben Breed's ship—twice as fast, and twice as easy to handle as our two-seater. An old Jenny, this ship was—with a new-type engine under the hood. And an all-metal prop.

At four thousand I looked over the side again. I stiffened in the cockpit. Back of the White House in Agua Prieta, in the yellow dust of the road, two men were spreading something— something white. A strip of cloth—a ground-strip!

I shouted back to Ben—pointed down. Then his voice came to me, steady.

"No good—the coin isn't there! I took it—look out, Mac! Dive her!"

A shape swooped down at us. Above the roar of the engine I could hear the crackling of machine-gun fire. A red stream flashed downward. A strut at the right spurted splinters. The fabric along the wing's leading edge was ripped badly. A wire snapped, curled inward shrilling fiercely.

Then I had the Jenny in a spin. The earth was whirling up to meet us. A shape dove down again from an angle, toward the spinning two-seater. Once more there came the staccato clatter of the Browning. My head was whirling. I was on the ragged edge. Glass on the instrument board was shattered as a bullet penetrated the front cockpit. It looked to me, in the flashing glimpses I could get, as though the right wing surface was warping. The wind was ripping the fabric more with each whirl. I could hardly see.

Killer above—or not—I had to get the controls in neutral, get the plane out of the spin. We were diving now—spinning no more. The earth was a black streak striking up at us. I pulled back on the stick; the nose came up sluggishly. It came up too much. We almost went into a stall.

Breed's voice came to me, from the rear cockpit.

"Steady—nose her down, Mac! We're south of Prieta—it's a level stretch. Land her—then do as I say!"

I tried to ask where the Wop's ship was, couldn't get the words clear enough. The two-seater was diving again. Breed's voice came more clearly.

"He's roaring my ship westward—almost out of sight. Sure he got us—watch her, Mac! Got to get down alive—"

Mesquite and sand rushed up at us. We struck heavily, bounced. I nosed her over to hold flying speed. We struck again. The landing gear cracked. This time we stayed down. The nose dug in, the prop splintered. I could feel the tail whipping up and over. Then there was a crash, and my arms were before my face, trying to protect it.

My left side took a battering. I could hear the hiss of water from the radiator, hitting the hot engine, the exhaust pipes. Something was lifting me clear of the plane—an arm. There was a red glare before me now. I was being dragged away from it. I could hear heavy breathing. My eyes cleared—Breed was half dragging me, half carrying me away from the burning plane. We were on a slope—that made the going hard. A short distance ahead was foliage, fairly heavy. Breed was heading for it. I limped along. And then we were down, out of sight. The fire got to the gas tank—there was a booming explosion. Black smoke spurted up into the sky. We lay in silence for several minutes. Ben Breed spoke first.

"Bum coin, Mac—Johnny Green planted a stack of it for me, early this morning. Got him out of the hospital after I got you back to the hotel. He went across and stuck the green and yellow stuff in the phonograph horn at the White House. In the big room, not the little one. Figured the fake stuff would help. May trace 'em that way. And things looked tough. I sighted Cards Ganlin in town."

I stared at Ben Breed. His gray eyes were squinted; there was a cut under his left eye. The bandage on his wrist was loose. He looked tired, all in.

"The ground-strip didn't mean anything to the Wop," I said slowly. "He was for shooting us out of things, anyway."

Breed nodded. "You know a lot, Mac," he said quietly. "He figured you were playing in with me. I wasn't so sure of that. Had a hunch you might be sitting in with the Wop's outfit. So I played you from both ends. Cards Ganlin got my ship from Lew Grey. Grey put up a fight, but it didn't do any good. They transferred the coin in this Douglas job to the single-seater. Then Ganlin tried to play it solo-like, and you heard what the Wop said. He's out. Flores has got my ship—and he's heading westward. But it's just the beginning, Mac. The game's big and—"

"The ninety thousand—" I said slowly—"what about *it?*"

"Deposited in the bank they robbed, in my name," Ben stated slowly. "Got it from your body, after, you went out. They forced Juan to drug your gin, but they slipped up, in some way, on my ginger ale, I got the belt inside my shirt—and fought it out. When the Wop discovers the coin his men got is bum—he'll be sore. He may figure a double-cross. He may figure some Mex in Agua Prieta got the real stuff. We stay out of sight—and wait. He'll come back. Or he'll send someone, and we can pick up the trail. He's not through with us, Mac."

I grinned weakly. Ben Breed closed his eyes. The fabric of the plane was crackling. And that was about the only sound we could hear.

"He'll be just as tough when he comes back, Bennie," I stated slowly. "First blood—for him."

Breed half opened his eyes. His lips held a cold smile. He spoke huskily.

"It's the *last* blood that counts, Mac," he returned quietly.

Blue Murder

The Wop and his gang of knifemen and gunmen were smearing the Border town with their own brand of hold-up, robbery, and murder—Border Brand, as it is called by Mac, the ex-flier, who is sitting in with Ben Breed to get the killer and take him across the Line for justice to work upon.

SATURDAY NIGHT, AROUND ten o'clock. The *Avenida* was crowded with humans. And all of these humans would stay across the Line until it got light—most of them in Tia Juana. The Border closed at six in the evening; it was a tough Line to squeeze across when it was not supposed to be open. I knew that, because I'd tried that little stunt once. It hadn't been a success.

From where I was standing I could see the front part of the Foreign Club. It was a square to the southward—a low, rambling building filled with gaming tables of all sorts. Roulette, twenty-one, stud-poker, dice games—and the longest bar in that section of the country, which is saying something. Less than an hour ago I'd spent half that length of time wandering around the interior of the place. And the human I had been looking for had failed to show.

That was all right, too. The Foreign Club is just *one* of the gambling places in about the toughest town in Baja California. There were others—plenty of them. I was just doing the job thoroughly—according to my idea—and looking for my man where he might be if he were dumb. Tonight—he wasn't dumb.

I stood in the doorway of the Green Tunnel. There was nothing about the shack that resembled a tunnel, and there was nothing about it that was green—except the beer the Mex bartenders shoved across the slippery wood. In the rear of the place, which fronted for about six feet on the *Avenida*, a giant negro was playing the "Memphis Blues" on a piano that sounded as if it hadn't been tuned since the piece had been written—and which probably hadn't. At intervals, voices, raised drunkenly, drowned out the tinny sound.

It had been raining heavily. Now there were stars in the sky. It was warm. There was mud on the not-so-good paving of the *Avenida*, pulled in by the passage of cars over the dirt from the Border inspection shacks, a half mile from the town. Coming in, the inspection shacks hadn't bothered me. I'd flown across, at the ceiling of the two-seater, which was around eleven thousand. The ship was down twelve miles southeast of the town, and I'd come in with a dead engine. Maybe someone had heard the wire shrill—more likely they hadn't. I'd almost cracked up in the landing, but it hadn't been the first time I'd set my ship down on the same stretch of sand and mesquite. There wasn't a shack within three miles of the spot where the two-seater rested. I'd hiked the twelve miles into Tia Juana. That was that.

I looked a lot like most of the humans walking the *Avenida*— pretty tough. Ten days had passed since Ben Breed, the Federal op, and myself had tangled with the Wop, and had come out a poor second. Or maybe not such a poor second—that depends on how you figure it. But when a guy sticks up a bank in Wheeler, Utah—flies to the Border town of Douglas, Arizona—and then loses the ninety grand he's killed two men to get, he's pretty sure to be sore. The Wop had been sore. He'd pulled a fast one on Ben and myself—with his gang he'd stuck up a Douglas bank and grabbed off thirty grand. At first they'd had the figure up a bit. But thirty was right. He'd crashed us down across the Line—and winged the ship he'd stolen from Ben toward Tia Juana. Toward Mexicali or Calexico, or a lot of other places, for that matter. But we figured on Tia Juana. Ben

did, anyway, and he has a habit of figuring right once in a while. After the crash we'd laid low, drinking a few in Agua Prieta on the fact that we hadn't been killed in the drop. We thought maybe the Wop would come back for the ninety grand. We thought wrong.

So here I was in Tia Juana, with a beard on my rather lean face, along with a lot of dirt. And the gent I was looking for wasn't the Wop. He was a bird named O'Leary. One of the most important jobs in O'Leary's life was to get information to Ben Breed. He'd got some. Some days ago Ben had started for Tia Juana. His instructions were that if I didn't hear from him in four days I was to fly down, land out from the town, come in and look for O'Leary. I hadn't heard from Ben.

A blonde who was close to fifty and trying to look close to sixteen stopped in front of me. She smiled, and I couldn't say much for her bridge work. She started to say something that I'd heard a dozen times in the last hour. I shook my head.

"I'm from Brooklyn—and I'm a good boy," I stated, and reached for another pill.

She grinned. "The hell you say!" she returned in a voice that hadn't been improved much by bum whiskey. "I used to go to church there."

I nodded. It was a cinch that I couldn't waste time listening to the usual sob story. And besides, I was getting a glimpse of somebody that might be my man, across the *Avenida*. He was limping along near the gutter, and he wore a battered straw hat. I started to move out. The girl—letting it go at that—grabbed me by the arm.

"Nothing doing!" I snapped, and started to move again.

"Ben's sick," she said slowly. "Try Pedro, at the 'Frisco House."

That straightened me up. The girl's fingers slipped away from my arm—three or four men came out through the Green Tunnel's doorway, with a rush. I was shoved one way—the girl the other. There was a jam on the narrow sidewalk. Everybody was talking loudly—almost everybody was drunk. There was a shrill scream—not far away. The crowd was milling around now; I got out of it, headed across the street. I looked for my man—he was out of sight. I swore softly. A khaki-clad Mex cop was running up the street. He headed in toward the crowd. I hesitated. There had been a familiar note about that scream. Listen to some women talk and you get an idea what they'd sound like if they were to yell. I moved back across the street.

The crowd was widening out a little. The Mex cop was jabbering in his own particular language. I stared down at the figure stretched out on the wet paving. One glance was enough. The lady who had gone to church in Brooklyn was through doing a lot of things she had done in the past. There was a red blot over her throat; it was spreading.

I turned away. Someone had stuck a knife in her throat. And

she hadn't yelled like that *after* the striking had been done. That meant she'd recognized someone. She'd guessed what was coming.

Ben was sick—that was what she had said. And I was to "try" Pedro, at the 'Frisco House. I lighted a pill from the stub of the old one. There had been that rush out of the Green Tunnel. Maybe that hadn't meant a thing. And maybe it had. Then the lady from Brooklyn had gone down—and out. The point was—had anyone seen her talking to me? That is, anyone who counted?

I moved along the *Avenida* on the opposite side of the street from which I had been standing. The crowd was getting thicker on the other side. Another khaki-clad Mex cop appeared. He was short and fat. He waddled toward the crowd, disappeared.

The soiled Panama I wore was pulled pretty far down over my eyes—I reached up and pulled it down some more. I muttered grimly:

"The Wop's in town. Things are starting to happen. Time for a drink."

The easiest thing to get in Tia Juana is a drink. The place I wandered into had some sort of a Mex name. There were smeared pictures of bulls and toreadors on the walls. This time it was a Mex who was playing a tinny piano. There was a small dance floor in the rear. I got a foot on the rail and ordered a gin fizz. The bird who waited on me had been a bum pug some years ago. He had tin ears, a flattened nose and thick lips. He looked Irish, I tossed over a half dollar.

"The 'Frisco House, Cap—where is she?" I asked, and pulled a noisy yawn to show that it wasn't at all important.

The ex-pug grinned, showing that he hadn't had much of a defense for his teeth. He spoke thickly.

"A half mile south of town, on the road to Ensenada. Don't go out before it gets light."

I took a swallow of the fizz. "How come?" I asked. "Someone going to do something to someone?"

The ex-pug nodded. "Make it plural—an' you've got the dope," he returned.

I finished off the fizz. Some gent alongside of me was howling for a beer. I sized the ex-pug up as he filled the order. He didn't look like a human who would talk just to hear the words come out. I slipped a ten spot across the bar. The ex-pug inspected it critically. Then he nodded his head.

"What do I answer?" he asked in his hoarse voice.

"The dope on the 'Frisco House," I returned, grinning.

He leaned forward across the bar. There was a lot of racket in the place.

"Pedro Guerra runs the shack," he stated. "He's a sawed-off Mex who likes plenty of women around. He used to tend bar here. Another guy took a lady out there a few days ago. Pedro didn't like the other guy—an' he did like the lady. He slips this other guy some knock-out stuff, and kicks him out. Tonight this bird comes in here with a couple of pals. They drink beer, instead of the real stuff—an' talk cold like. The guy that was tossed out of the 'Frisco House had a bum watch, an' he keeps lookin' at it. After a while they go out—maybe ten minutes ago."

I nodded. "You know the guy they tossed out?" I asked.

The ex-pug shook his head. But he was a rotten liar. He steered me off.

"Got a woman friend out there. She give me the stuff," he replied.

I nodded again. "Maybe this guy was short and thick-set," I suggested. "Half Mex and half wop. Maybe his first name was Antonio, eh?"

The bartender shrugged his shoulders. He might have figured that I had another ten spot. I had, but it was staying with me. I knew enough.

The ex-pug reached for my empty drink glass. A tall, thin individual with red hair came in the door of the place. He was smoking a black-papered cigarette. He headed straight for me. I let my left hand stay on the bar—but not my right. The tall bird gave the ex-pug a funny grin. Or maybe it wasn't funny.

"Who was the lady I seen you with last night, Brick?" he asked in a knife-edged tone.

The bartender sort of stiffened. He got white around the lips. The tall guy was my idea of a tough egg. I kept my right hand inside the pocket of my khaki pants. Red was plenty cool, and he was talking nonsense that wasn't nonsense. Not to Brick, anyway.

"No come-back for that one, eh?" Red sort of laughed. Like his voice, it was knife-edged—that laugh. "All right, Brick. Only—she had an accident. Throat trouble. If she talks any more, Brick, it sure will be funny!"

I got it then. And Brick got it. Mechanically he handed the tall bird a bottle and a whiskey glass. His face was a sickly white. I strolled away from the bar. Out near the door I stopped. The Mex had been playing some sort of a march. He stopped in the middle of it. Stopped the fast stuff and started to play something a lot different. Blue stuff—slow and draggy. The "Memphis Blues."

Three Mexicans came in from the street. They were dressed

in rough clothes, and they were making a lot of noise, staggering. But I noticed that they staggered in the general direction of the tall, thin, red-headed bird. There were some tables near the entrance to the place, over in a corner. I grabbed a seat in one, with my back against the wall. Some more greasers came in. The place was crowding up. There was a lot of shouting. The Mex at the piano was dragging out the blues.

Then it sounded. It had a pop-whish sound, a lot like champagne being uncorked. Only this wasn't the sort of place where champagne was sold over the bar. Not even Mex champagne. There was a hoarse, guttural shout—then a crash. I muttered slowly:

"Last count for Brick!"

There was a rush for the door. It was a drunken rush. But most of the drunks were cold sober. The Mex at the piano had stopped playing the blue stuff. He was back at the march again. I let my head slop over on my arms, but kept my eyes opened. The tall, red-headed bird walked out of the place. He turned to the left, and he didn't look back. I got up, went over to the bar. Three of the four bartenders were standing pretty stiff—and looking toward the spot where I'd last seen the ex-pug standing. He wasn't in sight, and their eyes slanted downward.

I went out. The red-headed bird was moving pretty fast toward the Foreign Club. Across the street a guy was limping. He wore a battered straw hat. The same fellow I'd seen a few minutes ago. But I was playing things differently now. A lady from Brooklyn had told me something—and then she'd stopped talking. I'd bought some information from an ex-pug, and he'd never spend that ten spot. The bird with the limp and the battered hat was too much in my sight.

I let him go, and trailed the redheaded one. And I began to worry about Ben Breed. The wire he'd sent had been in code. I'd never seen O'Leary, but he'd wired that my man would have a battered straw hat, a limp—and a bandage around his left wrist. I was to get in his way, and let O'Leary talk first. Somehow, right now I didn't feel like getting in O'Leary's way. And I commenced to think that maybe Ben *was* sick. Or worse.

One thing was sure—there was some smoothly-pulled, nicely-organized murder going on. And it all seemed to happen while draggy music was being pounded on tinny pianos.

I kept my man in sight. He was moving more slowly now. It was my guess that Red had a gun, with a silencer, in his pocket. I didn't think that he'd finished the girl. He wasn't Mex enough to handle a knife that way. I thought under my breath:

"Maybe I *don't* figure, at that. The girl was Brick's woman out at the 'Frisco House. She talked to Brick. The guy that Pedro kicked out found out about that. So the two of them went where talking may not do so much harm. That's all."

But I wasn't kidding myself. There was plenty of reason for the Wop wanting to finish me off—and not before he gave me the chance to answer some of his questions. Perhaps Red didn't know me. Perhaps he did.

There was a muddy street, unpaved, running east and west— just north of the Foreign Club. The red-headed one turned westward on the street. I followed, keeping close to the frame shacks along the street, all of which were bars. There wasn't much of a crowd.

I heard something that stiffened me a bit. It was distant, faint. It was a drone—a sky drone. The hum of a plane's engine, when that plane is high in the sky. I stepped back a few feet into a muddy alley. But I didn't tilt my head right away. The alley was black, and I listened. Some times the other fellow forgets to hold his breath. Everything seemed all right. I tilted my head.

The drone was still very faint. That ship had altitude. And I guessed that her pilot was circling—circling over Tia Juana. Once, I thought a couple of stars were blotted out by a shape, but I wasn't sure. And the sky drone probably wouldn't have been noticed by the average person. A pilot's ears get accustomed to even the distant exhaust roar of a pulling engine.

The night wasn't black, but the stars weren't bright enough to show up that plane, and there was no moon. I stepped out into the street again—and swore softly. Red color vanished from the mud. But out in the middle of the street was a glow—a glow of blue. It colored the 'dobe shacks, the frame ones. It daubed the mud with blue. Mexicans were grinning and staring at it. I was staring at it, but not grinning. To me it wasn't just some drunken fool's idea of a celebration with fireworks. That blue flare was a signal—a signal to the pilot of that ship high in the sky!

I moved along the mud. A dirty-faced, skinny wreck of a man was close beside me now. He was bent over badly, there was a scar running from the left corner of his lips to his left ear. He shuffled when he walked. The flare in the street was hissing, dying in color. A voice sounded, very low.

"Follow me, Mac—when I turn in keep going. Look for red light in front of Mex 'dobe shack. You go inside. Walk slow—I'll be there."

Ben Breed! I reached for a pill, my fingers shaking a bit. Husky-voiced, but as cool as ever. And he wasn't sick, or out at the 'Frisco House. He was moving slowly along the mud, back toward the *Avenida*. Just one of the hundred or so of old wrecks in Tia Juana.

I moved after him. The blue flare had died; the drone of the ship in the sky was dying. The crowd grew thicker as we neared the *Avenida*—the town's main street. I lost sight of Breed's bent form, had a little flash of panic, then found him again. We crossed the street, kept heading eastward. I smiled grimly. No fooling Ben; my pulled down Panama, beard and dirty face hadn't stopped him from picking me up, even on a street unlighted except for the flare.

Blue again. Luck—or something else? An odd sort of a color for a flare. Red or green or yellow—that would have been more like it. I strained my ears. The sky drone had ended. The pilot of the plane had picked up the color of the flare—had winged away. In what direction—and why?

That was the big thing—why the signal? Was it because there had been a double kill? I doubted that. It didn't seem to me that the lady from Brooklyn or the bartender were that important. Perhaps it meant that something had been cleared up—it had been a come-in signal.

My eyes went to Ben Breed's bent figure. As I watched him he turned toward the left. He entered a large, well-lighted saloon. I kept straight on, walking slow. A hundred feet down was a red light. The crowd was thinning again. Get away from the *Avenida* a square or so and the town's deserted, dark—and dangerous. That thought gave me a kick. It was bad enough *on* the main street.

I turned in at the red light. There were battered stairs, leading upward. Slipping my right hand inside my coat pocket, I started up. There was no hurry. From somewhere above there came the squeal of a soprano on a phonograph record. I stopped, listened. It was high-brow stuff, opera. I went on.

The stairs ended on a dimly-lighted landing. There was a door, half closed. The room was poorly lighted, too. I got a boot against the door, shoved it. There are two or three *bad* ways of entering a strange room. I wasn't using any of them. A voice said:

"Come on, Mac—O'Leary's down below."

The voice was low, and it was Ben Breed's. I went into the room. It was very small. There was a table and two stools—and another door not quite opposite the one through which I entered. Ben was seated on a stool, facing the door I'd kicked. There was a pack of Mex pills on the table. He grinned at me. I turned toward the door.

"Let it stay open," he said slowly. "We need air."

I dropped on the other stool; Ben shoved over the cigarettes. A kerosene lamp hung from the ceiling; by its light I could see that Breed's eyes looked pretty tired. But their gray had a hard expression, too—as he narrowed them on mine.

"How long have you been in, Mac?" he asked quietly.

I told him. He nodded. "Anything funny happen?" he asked grimly.

"Depends on your sense of humor, Ben," I stated. "A woman got a knife through her throat—and a man took some lead. In both cases I was pretty close when things happened. The woman stated that you were sick. She suggested that I try Pedro, at the 'Frisco House. The man told me about the love affairs of a couple of Mex boys. Then he got his. He advised me to stay *away* from the 'Frisco House."

Ben Breed pulled on his pill. "The Wop's here, Mac," he said slowly. "I haven't seen him—but he's here. Pedro Flores, out at the 'Frisco House—that's his brother. Maybe I get the tense wrong. Maybe it should be—Pedro *was* his brother."

I stared at Ben. There was a little silence, which was broken by the playing of "Oh You Beautiful Doll" on the phonograph.

"If Pedro's finished off," I said, "I'll lay a bet he went out to the tune of 'Memphis Blues'."

Ben Breed shook his head. "No piano out there," he stated slowly.

I sat up straight. Ben knew plenty. He leaned across the table.

"Been trailing you for thirty minutes, Mac. Was in on both those kills. Know who ran the jobs?"

I made a guess. "Tall, thin bird—with red hair and a cold voice."

"Right," Ben stated. "And his name is Ganlin—'Cards' Ganlin."

I swore softly. Ganlin was the bird the Wop had tried to make me believe Ben Breed had been, back at Douglas ten days ago. And the guy he'd claimed to have bumped off for trying to double-cross him. I stared at Ben.

"Sure?" I snapped.

Breed grunted. His gray eyes went toward the opened door.

"Positive," he stated. "Cards is here gunning for the Wop—and the Wop knows he's here, now. That's the way Cards is playing it. He hates the Wop's insides. Know why?"

I shook my head. Ben spoke in a low voice. His eyes were on mine again.

"Up the Line, at Laredo, they both fell for the same woman. She was a small-time actress, stranded in Laredo. A wise lady, I suppose. Anyway, she played them both. Then when she got all she wanted from the Wop—she dropped him. Cards was making a move; they were watching his gambling too close up that way. He took the frail along, and neither of them told the Wop about it. He got sore, picked up the chase at Juarez. One night he walked into a room in that town, a back room of a gambling joint. The girl was playing blue songs on a piano— for Cards. He liked that sort of music. A couple of the Wop's men grabbed the gambler, stood him up against the wall. The Wop stood near the door, and let the blue-playing lady have a gun-full of lead. Now she's playing her blues wherever such ladies go to play them. The Wop dropped Cards that night with his gun butt. It wasn't so long ago—maybe three weeks. Now they're both in town together."

I did some thinking. The bartender hadn't told me such a truthful story about the 'Frisco House. But he'd had the right idea, anyway. Two crooks out to get each other. And the lady from Brooklyn—

Ben Breed lighted one cigarette from the tip of his last. He spoke quietly.

"There's something on, Mac—besides a few killings. The Wop knows you're in town. The lady who talked to you happened to be the one who was keeping house for his brother Pedro. They had you spotted, and she pulled the job of giving you a bum tip. I was close enough to you to stop you from acting foolish—but you didn't act that way. Maybe it was because Cards started to kill. Someone was playing the blues inside the Green Tunnel. Cards didn't use the knife. But he *did* walk in on the bartender across the street. He had a Mex planted at the piano. Blues again—and Cards used a silenced gun to pop his man out. Brick Casey was an undercover man for Pedro Flores. Last night he was out walking with the lady who talked to you."

I swore softly, remembering Cards Ganlin's words of greeting to the bartender. "Who was the lady I seen you with last night, Brick?" And that icy cold voice of his.

Suddenly I stiffened in the seat. "What's the game on the kills?" I asked. "Ganlin trying to pay the Wop back in his own coin? Using this blue song stuff to remind him of what he did up at Juarez?"

Ben Breed's voice was suddenly husky. It hadn't been, when he'd last spoken. There were foot-falls on the stairs. Ben said:

"Don't turn, Mac—I'll take this chap. O'Leary's down below. No, it isn't just Cards trying to get back. Something bigger than that. Trying to break his nerve, maybe. See it? Two of the Wop's outfit gone now—both while the blues have been banged out on—"

Ben stopped talking. His gray eyes were narrowed. The foot-falls were louder now—but we both heard something else. A hissing of breath that almost amounted to sobbing.

I didn't turn. Ben Breed was the big boss. He knew his stuff. The foot-falls ceased; I heard the breath-sobbing almost behind me. Ben was half out of his chair. A voice sounded, broken, laboring.

"Got me—half square down—the Wop's flying out of—"

I turned then. A figure had been gripping the door with both hands—now the grip weakened. The figure crashed heavily to the floor. I started up from the stool. Ben spoke sharply.

"Shut the door, Mac—snap that bolt! Make it fast!"

I had to shove the legs of the one who had fallen out of the way—to close the door. I slipped the bolt. Then I turned toward

Ben Breed. I remembered that he'd told me to leave the door opened.

"O'Leary?" I asked grimly.

Ben shook his head. "Never saw him before, Mac. Yet he finds us up here—"

He stopped, straightened. I swore fiercely. The phonograph had been silent. Now it started to wail again. It filled the room, seeming to come from somewhere in the back of the shack. And the record being played was the "Memphis Blues"!

Seconds passed—not too many of them. Ben spoke.

"Three for Cards. But the Wop knows we're up here. He sent this guy to frame us. Follow me—don't talk. Keep fingers on your rod. When we get outside get away from me. Head for the Foreign Club. Buy a drink at the bar. I'll be in—stay there until I come. And watch yourself."

I nodded. Ben Breed slipped open the door back of his stool. He went out, downward. I followed. Back of us the phonograph wailed on.

"Blue murder!" I muttered to myself. "Each time the kill's a little closer."

AT THE BOTTOM of the stairs Ben moved out through a narrow doorway that had no door. I let him get a little ahead. When I stepped through the doorway he was out of sight. I was in a noisy, well-lighted saloon and dance place. The one into which Ben had turned from the street. I moved toward the door, keeping my eyes open—and doing some more thinking. The bird who had collapsed up above—he had got out one broken sentence of importance. Something about the Wop flying out. I thought of the blue flare. Scared? Antonio Flores yellow? I doubted that.

Anyway, it was a Cards Ganlin kill. That gave me something else to think about. Ben Breed hadn't known the one who had got up the stairs, spoken his piece—and crashed out. Ganlin had, as I saw it. One of the Wop's boys, and yet he gave Ben Breed information about the guy we were looking for. Like hell he did! Not straight stuff, that was sure.

I reached the street, headed for the Foreign Club. Back on the jammed *Avenida* again, crossing it. The parking place in front of the Club was almost empty of cars. Americans cleared out of Tia Juana before six. It was the foreign crowd, and the cheap crooks who stuck now. Not the big ones. The little ones—the fellows that the U.S.A. government didn't figure it worth while to come across after.

The Wop knew all this. He knew that Ben Breed was over to get him, to take him back across the Line. And he knew that Ben wouldn't be particular in the manner of the taking. Once back in the States—and caught—it was the rope or the chair for Antonio Flores. Depending upon the State that got him.

I smiled grimly as I headed toward the doors of the Foreign Club. The Wop was fighting now. Fighting Ben Breed—and Cards Ganlin. But that didn't mean that Antonio was licked. Half Mex, half Italian—he was a tough character. After the Douglas affair— I should know. And I did know.

Inside the Club I moved toward the bar. The place wasn't crowded, but there were plenty playing the games. I ordered up a gin fizz. Then I got my back to the bar, and looked the humans over. They were a fine bunch of thugs. Most of them were playing at the roulette games, with a lot trying to beat the dice. My eyes went to the door. Ben Breed was walking in. He wore an ancient sheep-skin coat and an old felt hat. The face scar was gone; he was pretty clean. Ben Breed—playing it straight!

He spotted me right away, headed toward the bar. He looked thinner than ever, and he was walking with his natural stoop. Thin—but wiry, Ben was. And he *could* handle a gun.

I turned my back to the big room, and waited for him to reach me. He came up on my left, ordered a beer. Then he spoke, in a low voice. There was such a babble of sound in the room it was difficult for me to hear him.

"O'Leary's gone," he stated. "Chances are he'll be picked up in a gutter or a back room, done in. Things are getting tight."

I said nothing. Ben was frowning. He finished half the beer.

"A plant, Mac," he stated. "The Wop is still sticking in town. He's out for Cards now. It's a finish fight. See our play?"

I grinned. "If Cards gets the Wop—that's all right," I stated. "But if the Wop gets Ganlin—"

"—we grab him off at the kill," Ben finished. "That is—we do if we're alive."

I grinned on. Ben finished the beer. I spoke again.

"How about that ship, Ben?" I asked. "And the flare Cards touched off?"

He swore softly. "You missed that one, Mac," he stated. "Cards didn't touch it off. A Mex staggered out from the *Red Mill*, across the street, acted drunk as hell—and touched her off. Ganlin ducked—I was watching the Mex, and lost him."

I grunted. "Plant to make us believe that bird who went out up in the room!" I muttered. "We'd heard the ship, seen the flare. The Wop figured we'd slide out of town—fly across after him."

Ben lighted a pill. "Maybe so," he stated. "Maybe not. Cards is playing it hard. He never had red hair—until I spotted him yesterday. He's dyed it. Figures he'll fool the Wop. So far— yes. The local police are making it easier for him now. They're getting excited. They're used to murders in town. But most of them are cheap—and the reasons plain. This is getting tough. They're hauling in some of the Wop's boys. He's been in town longer than Cards Ganlin. He's got relations here that the *officios* know about. Up to him to work fast. He's got to get Cards in a hurry—or break for it."

I nodded. Ben faced around slowly, He gripped me by the arm.

"Ganlin!" he whispered. "Don't rush the turn around!"

I yawned, dropped my pack of pills, turned and picked it up. Ben was leaning heavily on the bar. His head was lolling around like a drunken man's. His gray eyes were half closed. My own eyes went toward the main entrance of the Club.

The icy-voiced, red-headed individual who had talked grim comedy at Brick was coming down an aisle between the gambling tables. His left hand played with a cigarette; his right was out of sight. His eyes moved all over the room as he headed for the bar.

I muttered to Ben:

"Wise guy. A safe place for him to get a drink. The Wop won't come in here."

Ben Breed started to sing thickly. There were several reasons why I figured the Wop wouldn't try the Foreign Club. It was the showy gambling place of Tia Juana. And it was watched pretty closely by Federal Government men—Mex government—who would have no particular hesitation in grabbing off the Wop. I doubted if he had an "in" at Tia Juana.

Cards Ganlin got about fifty feet from the bar—before I stiffened, swore sharply. Back of him, beside a roulette table from which he had just stepped into sight, stood the Wop! His head was bent slightly forward, something glittered in his right hand. I saw the gun come up.

Crack! No silencer on the Wop's gun. The sound of it filled the place. Cards Ganlin stiffened, swung as his body slumped toward the wood of the floor. Then, suddenly every light in the place went out!

Ben Breed stopped playing drunk. His left hand gripped my left wrist.

"This way!" he snapped, and we started to move. "One of Flores' men—pulled a switch!"

Confusion? There was plenty of it. Voices shouting hoarsely. Men yelling for lights, cursing. The place was in blackness. But Ben Breed seemed to know where he was going. The fingers of his left hand gripped my wrist tightly—he led me along. Figures bumped against us, voices shouted in our ears. And then we were outside. There was light from the street—the *Avenida*.

"Worked wrong for us!" I muttered. "The Wop got—"

I stopped. A man was running, bent over and in zig-zag fashion, toward the muddy street that crossed the *Avenida*. I got a glimpse of the man's left arm, hanging loosely at his side as he ran. And his hair was red.

"Cards!" Ben Breed snapped. "The Wop was shaky—didn't finish him."

I stared at the running figure. Breed was watching the main entrance of the Club; we had come out through a side door. The Wop came into sight. His gun was still gripped in his hand.

He raised it now. Ben Breed's right came out of a pocket of his sheepskin coat.

Something hissed through the air—we both ducked. A knife clattered against the frame-work of the Club. Ben whirled; his gun cracked. A Mex near the corner of the building pitched forward, his hands going to his right knee. He cried out hoarsely.

The Wop didn't fire. Ganlin was lost in the crowd now. Men were running toward the Foreign Club—but not very many of them. The majority were getting in the clear. Ben Breed snapped words at me.

"Cover that Mex on the ground—"

I half turned. A flivver was rattling in through the parking space. I got my automatic leveled on the Mex, who was groaning and gripping his leg. There was the *crack* of a gun—splinters spurted out from the wood of the building. Then Ben's gun sounded.

The flivver splashed mud—a figure leaped toward it. Ben's gun spoke again. He called to me sharply.

"Come on!"

I followed him around a side of the building. There was a gray, closed car standing in the mud back of the Club. Beside it stood a man with a battered straw hat on his head. His face was brown, but he wasn't Mex.

"O'Leary!" Ben's voice held a surprised note. He turned to me. "Tell him how to drive for the plane. All right—pile in! Back seat!"

We piled in. Ben and myself in the rear seat. I told the driver how to go—out the Ensenada road six miles. Slope with mesquite on the crest—turn there to the left, inland, away from the Pacific. The car jerked into motion.

Ben spoke. We were both leaning forward, gripping the back of the front seat.

"Thought they got you, Mike—a bird crashed in on us—"

The driver cut in. His voice was short and sharp.

"Mex cop started to take me away—got me a couple of blocks off, and I made a break for it. Slammed him down. When I got back to the red light there was a crowd outside. A lot of shooting inside. Figured you were out of the place— headed for the car."

Ben Breed nodded. His voice was grim.

"Cards had the Wop's man knifed—the bird who was coming up to give us a bum steer. Then the Wop came along to finish things up. Must have put lead into that room without waiting to see who was inside. Open her up, Mike—got to make that ship before—"

Ben stopped. I snapped at him.

"Before *what?*"

Breed smiled grimly. "Before the Wop gets clear in the one he stole from me!" he replied.

I stared at him. We were riding the Ensenada road now, and the rains had made her bad. There was no sign of the flivver. Ben spoke jerkily.

"That flare—signal for the Wop to come in. He was—across the Line. Someone thought they had Ganlin lined for him. Had—I guess. He almost went out. Unless I'm wrong—the Wop set his ship down close in to Tia. We've got to ride like hell to stop him—"

The car skidded dangerously around a curve. The road was bad—the rest of the country was dry. Sand and mesquite. Mountains to the right—the Cocopahs.

"Got the Browning mounted?" Ben snapped.

I nodded my head. "Under cover in the rear cockpit," I returned. "We tackle him—in the air?"

"Over *California* ground," he came back. "And that means we've got to be up above, waiting for him. He's got a faster ship."

I groaned. "Maybe he won't take off," I stated. "He'll hear our engine—"

"His own will drown ours," Ben came back. "He had his chance at Ganlin—missed. The town won't hold both of them. The Wop's looking for an out. Ganlin's too strong here. Up the Line—it's different."

We were traveling. We came to the road that led toward the two-seater. It was a bad road—we slowed down. Ben Breed swore grimly.

"Flores is slippery," he muttered. "We had a good chance to grab him here—and we've still got some of it left. If we lose him—

A tire blew. The driver jerked his head. He had blue eyes, an Irish nose—and the complexion of a pock-marked Mex. He started to ask a question, but Ben cut him off.

"Run on the rim!" he snapped.

We did. It made the going rougher, but not much slower. I thought of something else.

"Maybe the Wop's nerve is shot. Maybe he's running wild—"

"He's got plenty of nerve left," Ben cut in. "He was thinking too much about—other things. That's why he missed Cards— missed killing him. At that, he hit him."

I nodded. We made a couple of miles in silence—conversational silence. The car was slipping all over the road, but she was getting nearer the two-seater all the time. Ben got his head close to O'Leary's right ear.

"If we get off all right in the ship—you drive back to Tia Juana. Keep moving around—and use your eyes. Hit the Foreign Club bar at twelve. If nothing happens, try the White House—at two. I'll get word to you, unless—"

Ben stopped. The road curved, and the car skidded in the mud. O'Leary was nodding his head. I thought of how close we'd come to going out—the last time we'd played the air game with the Wop. But I didn't say anything. *This* time we had a gun in the rear cockpit, and plenty of lead.

The car climbed a slope, started down the other side. The country was level, semi-desert ahead. I stared, made out the shape of the two-seater. She looked all right. Ben said:

"We'll drop off a quarter mile this side of her, Mike—you go on back. If anyone's found her that'll work out better."

O'Leary nodded again. The car was running on level road. He slowed her down. Ben spoke to me.

"You go in from the road—I'll cut across the sand, reach her from the other side. 'Bye, Mike!"

We were out of the car. I gripped my automatic in my right hand, ran with my body bent toward. Ben Breed was cutting across the mesquite and sand. There was no sign of anyone near the plane. I noted that the wind was as it had been when I had come down. The ship was headed into it. That would save time. Even a few seconds would count.

I took a chance—ran in pretty fast. Breed was heading in on the opposite side. The car was rattling back toward town. O'Leary was still riding on the rim. I jumped the wing-step. All clear in the rear cockpit. Getting a foot up front, I looked inside the front cockpit. Empty. Breed came up.

"I'll spin—the prop!" he breathed heavily. "Get inside!"

I slid into the seat, reached for my helmet and goggles. Then I snapped the switch. Ben Breed called out "Contact!" sharply. I nodded my head. He put his weight on the high blade of the prop, pulling her down. She didn't catch. He tried her again. This time the engine roared, the prop spun. I pointed out the stake ropes. Ben got them loose from the wing hoops, got the blocks from under the wheels. The engine was roaring steadily. I wiped my goggle-glass clear. Ben climbed into the rear cockpit, got the canvas off the gun. I told him where the goggles and helmet were.

He swung the Browning on the well-oiled bracket. I looked back, keeping the engine throttled down so that she wouldn't go over on her nose. In the dim light from the sky the barrel of the Browning looked more blue than black. It had a faint gleam—a blue gleam. Ben nodded his head.

"Right, MacLeod!" he snapped. "Let's go get this killer!"

I shoved forward the throttle. The engine of the two-seater wasn't any too warm, so I gave her a pretty long ground run. When I pulled back on the stick and she lifted clear of the sand and mesquite I breathed deeply. The field wasn't the best in the world. I climbed her toward Tia Juana in a mild glide. She was roaring smoothly. When I jerked my head again Ben Breed was sighting through the ring-rangers on the gun. I smiled grimly.

"That Browning—" I muttered— "can do some blue murder of her own!"

WE HAD THREE thousand, and were banking toward the west—when Ben gripped me by the right shoulder. I jerked my head. He had his left hand out in the prop-wash; a finger was pointing downward, to the west of the town.

I saw it right away—a red trail in the sky. The exhaust streak of a plane. It was low, and I couldn't see the ship, but the trail was slanting. The plane was climbing. And she was heading straight toward Port San Ysidro, the little town on the American side of the Line.

I banked the ship to the northward, cut the throttle and glided. That would take our own exhaust flame out of the air. It might prevent the Wop from spotting us. As I glided downward I stared over the side of the fuselage, watched the climbing ship. She was taking shape now. And she was a single-seater. Ben's old plane.

A voice sounded in my ears. "He's painted her wings—camouflaged her blue-gray! Mesquite and sand color!"

I nodded. My eyes went inside to the instrument on the dial board. With the engine cold I couldn't afford to glide her without giving her the gun once in a while. I shoved the throttle forward—the engine roared. Ben cried out.

"She's banking around! Spotted us by that flame, Mac!"

I stared. Sure enough—the little ship was heading back into Mexico, back over Tia Juana. The light from the town showed her up plainly as she winged almost parallel to the *Avenida*. And then she was out of the light glare—winging southward.

The two-seater went around in a vertical bank. I opened the engine wide, nosed her down a bit. We picked up speed. I jerked my head.

"Do we get her?" I shouted.

Ben nodded. I dove the two-seater more steeply. We were coming down in a wire-screaming roar now. And gaining rapidly on the other plane. But I knew that we would only have the one chance. Altitude was giving us the speed to catch her. In level flight she would wing away from us.

She was flying at about five hundred feet now, and not trying to get altitude. I jerked my head, saw that Ben Breed had the gun barrel out on the right side. I kept the two-seater on the left of the other ship. Ben's ship—she was. Yet after he squeezed the trigger of the Browning—

The Wop was a killer. A big-time killer. Even dead—he would be worth the price of a new plane for Ben Breed. We could fly him back across the Line. When the news finally got to the Mexican officials—they would be glad of it. It was an easy way out—for them. And maybe Ganlin would be glad, too.

We were within a hundred yards of the other plane now. She banked suddenly outward, away. I banked after her. Her nose came up—she zoomed. Then, suddenly, as I pulled the stick back and zoomed the two-seater, the little ship came out of her zoom, went over on a wing. I caught the lines of a prop-synchronized gun. There was the clatter of machine-gun fire.

The Wop was leading us too much. I banked to the left—then suddenly leveled off. From behind me came the sharp, staccato beat of the Browning. Red streamed out into the dark sky. I nosed the two-seater downward. Sand and mesquite came up—and the shape of the little ship flashed, going down in a slow spin. I held the two-seater in her dive.

The little ship came out of the spin. She was roaring southward, away from the town. One wing was drooping. Pulling back on the stick—I leveled our plane off, then went into a stiff dive. The little ship was less than fifty feet above the mesquite.

Her right wing was drooping badly. I jerked my head around, shouted at Ben above the wire shrill:

"He's going—to crash!"

Ben's face was grim. His lips were pressed closely together. We were coming down on the other plane again.

Suddenly her nose came up. Her prop made a slight circle of light. I swore softly, banked to the right, across her tail assembly. Red streaked up from her prop-synchronized gun. It was a close go. I zoomed the two-seater.

We came out of the zoom, leveled off. I shoved the throttle all the way forward. The Wop was putting up a fight—

Then the crash came. It reached my ears above the roar of the two-seater's engine. It was the ground smash of the little ship!

I stared down over the side. She was turning over against the side of a slope. Her tail assembly was whipping around. A wing collapsed—there was a cloud of sand as she dug in. I dove the two-seater for the nearest level stretch, stalled her down. She hit lightly, bounced once—rolled to a stop. By the time I got my safety belt snapped, got over the side—Ben Breed was running toward the other plane, gun in his hand. I started after him, leaving the prop of the two-seater spinning, throttled down.

The wreckage of the single-seater was burning. Suddenly I saw Ben pull up, go to his knees. A figure was staggering over a wing. Flames licked up the man. He was short, stocky. His right hand came up. Then his knees gave way under him. He went down near a clump of mesquite, rolled over on his back. Ben Breed straightened; we went up to him cautiously. The red glare from the ship struck his face.

My body went rigid. Ben swore in a strange, grim tone. *It was not the Wop!*

We stood for several seconds in silence. The flames crackled over the ship. Then Ben turned abruptly, moved toward the burning plane. The eyes of the one on the ground were wide, staring. He was Mex—and he looked something like the Wop. There were bullets in his chest—several of them.

Ben Breed came back. He spoke in a level, hard tone.

"Not my ship, Ben—and this is the Wop's brother. Pedro Flores!"

I swore softly. My eyes lifted. I grabbed Ben by the arm. There was a drone in my ears. A sky drone. It was very faint. We both stared toward the Line. Low in the sky was a faint trail of red. It slanted upward; already it was dying from sight. Ben spoke.

"The Wop, Mac! And he's across!"

I nodded, reached for a cigarette. My fingers were shaking pretty badly. A chase was hopeless. Once again the Wop was in the clear. Cards Ganlin had chased him out of Tia Juana—while we were sky-fighting his brother. Cards Ganlin—or fear of that gambler.

Ben Breed struck a match. We both lighted up. There was a little silence. The exhaust trail in the sky was very faint now. Ben Breed said:

"He won't let Ganlin get away with this. He's got a lot of men—up the Line. There'll be hell to pay—from now on. And he'll need money to fight Ganlin. That means—"

Ben stopped. But I knew what it meant. There were banks at Calexico, Juarez, Douglas, Nogales. The Wop would strike for the coin. Blue murder had driven him out of Tia Juana. Cards Ganlin was getting revenge—and letting the Wop know why.

"We'll fly out, Mac." Ben spoke quietly. "Head for Calexico.

I'll do some wire buzzing. There'll be hell popping now. The Wop's own brand."

"Border brand," I muttered.

Ben Breed was staring at the burning plane. I looked toward the northern sky. There was no drone of a ship in my ears now. But the rumble of the waiting two-seater was a slow beat. In it, I could hear a piano tinnily sounding—the blue stuff. I walked back toward the two-seater. Ben followed. They'd find Pedro Flores soon enough. The flames were a marker.

Ben Breed spoke slowly. He looked pretty tired, but his eyes were cold enough.

"Getting tight, Mac. If you don't want to stay in this thing—"

He saw what I thought of that suggestion. But I made it clearer in just one word. Ben grinned. We climbed into the two-seater, took off.

High Death

CALEXICO SWELTERED IN the heat of an August sun. Mexicali across the railroad tracks and the Line, sweltered also—and showed less signs of life. From where I sat, looking out of the dirtily-curtained window, the office of the *Jefe de Policia* could be seen. Two Mexicans, in soiled khaki shirts and pants, were talking listlessly near the entrance of the frame and adobe building. Shiny holsters, over their thighs, caught the glare of the sun. Both men were short and fat.

"The Wop's given us the slip," I muttered slowly. "And it's ten to one Gruttel won't show."

Ben Breed, sitting on the edge of the bed and smoking a Mex cigarette, moved one of his long arms.

"I'll take that bet," he stated in his hoarse voice. "Here's my one."

I fished out a damp ten spot, tossed it on the bed, beside Ben's buck. There was a rap on the door—a pause, two raps—another pause. Three raps. Ben slipped his right hand into the right pocket of his once-white pants, faced the door.

"All right, Murphy!" he called loudly. "Step in."

The door opened. Gruttel stepped inside, shut the door behind him. He was big-chested, husky. He had a square head and a fat, German face. His eyes were blue. He was breathing heavily, and his face was streaked with perspiration.

Ben Breed picked up my ten spot and his one—with his left hand. He slipped the bills into a pocket, spoke quietly to Gruttel.

"Where does he pull it—and when?" he asked, his gray eyes narrowing on the blue ones of the heated gentleman who had just come in.

Gruttel sucked in his breath. There was a sound outside, in the narrow corridor of the Red House. The sound gave Gruttel a jump. Ben spoke sharply.

"Keep your big feet on the floor! You been drinking over the Line?" It was quiet out in the corridor again. Gruttel turned his eyes toward Ben's. I got a glimpse of them. They were wide, held fear.

"I seen Bugs!" Gruttel's voice shook a bit. "He slid off the caboose of a freight."

I looked at Ben. "Bugs" Conroy had been out of the Big House four days. It was seven days since Cards Ganlin had chased the Wop out of Tia Juana, putting on his blue murder show. There had been a time when Conroy and the Wop were as close as a couple of Mexican fleas. And with Bugs on the outside again—

"Sure it was Conroy?" Ben snapped the question at Gruttel.

"Maybe you were seeing things."

Gruttel sprawled down into a battered chair. The muscles around his mouth jumped nervously.

"Don't I know that scar slantin' down from his left eye?" he muttered. "Didn't I put it there?"

I grinned. That was a tough one to beat. Ben Breed tossed a pack of pills across to Gruttel. The square-headed one reached for the pack. His fingers were shaking. He stiffened suddenly.

"Hell!" he muttered. "They're black!"

Ben's eyes narrowed. "Come up, Murphy!" he snapped. "You've smoked black-papered pills before. Want that century—or do you break for it now?"

Gruttel lighted the Mex pill. He inhaled deeply.

"I'm all right," he muttered. "Seein' Bugs gave me a jolt. I'm skippin' this country—and Mex, too. The hundred 'll get me to Colon. An' the Wop won't chase me that far. He played me dirty in Agua Prieta—he did. He's holdin' the cards right against his chest. No one gets a look—but him. I'm through."

Ben nodded. His gray eyes were smiling.

"Figured that, Gruttel. And I figured you'd know when Conroy was getting the warden's hand-shake. The Wop can use Bugs right now—use him more than he can you. Ganlin's riding him hard. The hundred's yours—here she is—"

Ben unfolded a soiled century spot. He held it loosely between a couple of his lean, left hand fingers. Gruttel's eyes widened. He spoke slowly.

"The job's for Friday—" his voice was lowered, almost a whisper—"and the bust is the Bisbee National. The Wop's got a plane on the north side of Mule Mountain—almost down the grade. The grab is for the Copper payroll. No time set. It's all on how things look. A couple of the boys are up there now—fixin' things easy. They're goin' to block the pass—both ways. That's all I got."

Ben's eyes were narrowed. He seemed to be looking beyond Gruttel. I was thinking fast. The Bisbee National. The copper town built almost on the top of Mule Mountain. A town sprawling along the road through the pass—all built on the two sides of the road. Just two ways out, down the side of Mule Mountain in each case. A sweet place for a stick-up, if the job were pulled right. And when the Wop pulled a job—

Ben Breed swore softly. He tossed the hundred dollar bill across to Gruttel.

"You're talking straight?" he snapped. "You're giving it to me right?"

The square-headed one leaned forward in the chair.

"Why not?" he snapped back. "Don't I hate the Wop's guts?"

Ben nodded slowly. I was watching Gruttel. He was folding the hundred spot with shaking fingers. Perspiration streaked the white skin of his face. Ben spoke slowly.

"If the Wop's holding the cards close—how come you're wise to the Bisbee deal, Murphy?"

My eyes went from Ben's to the blue ones of Gruttel. Ben had a habit of calling a human, whose name was not to be spoken too loudly, by the Irish tag of Murphy. From time to time these men Ben tagged Murphy passed out of the picture. Lead or a knife was generally the cause, and the passing was permanent.

Gruttel tried a smile that was almost a success. He reached for a dirty handkerchief, mopped his face.

"I went to the Wop, told him there was no sense of me stickin'—not with Bugs out. One of us would be lyin' flat in a hurry. Tony was wise to that fact. He gave me the layout, told me to hit it off for Bisbee—an' look things over. This was yesterday."

Ben nodded. "Yesterday—and where?" he asked slowly.

"Ticardi," Gruttel replied. "Little Mex village back of—"

"I know her," Ben cut in. "Watch yourself going out, Murphy. Where you catching the boat?"

"Ensenada," the square-headed one replied. "Got a kid down there—she likes me. If she's flush I'll take her along."

Ben nodded. Gruttel got to his feet. He slipped his right hand into a pocket of his soiled, light coat, moved toward the door of the room. He turned.

"I'm hopin' you grab the Wop off, Breed!" His voice was fierce. "If I didn't think you could—there'd be no squeal. He's a devil—that Mex! He's settin' to cut out Ganlin's heart—"

"Easy!" Ben spoke sharply. "Don't get yelling—not around here. So long, Murphy!"

Gruttel grinned weakly. He muttered something I didn't get. His eyes were at the crack of the slightly-opened door. He hesitated, got the door wide enough for his fat body, slipped through. The door closed gently behind him. Ben was frowning. He spoke grimly.

"Give you a chance, Mac. Ten to one they get him before he walks out on the street—there's the ten."

He tossed out my ten spot. I covered it with a silver dollar. We both sat quietly—waiting. Flies buzzed around the room. I turned, looked out of the window. A couple of minutes passed.

Gruttel walked into sight, moving toward the Line.

"You lose," I told Ben, and picked up the ten he'd won from me a few minutes before. "He gave you a lot of bunk for your hundred. The Wop would put that rat wise—like hell!"

Ben didn't say a thing. We were both watching Gruttel. He kept out in the middle of a dirty street. He kept looking around. There were frame houses on both sides. Everything was very quiet outside. And then, suddenly, it wasn't quiet. Guns clattered sharply from two directions—and they sounded like shoulder submachine-guns!

Gruttel went down to his knees. He got up right away, screaming hoarsely. He tried to reach the left side of the street. The clatter sounded again. The square-headed one sprawled out, rolled over on his face, lay motionless. The two Mexicans in front of the Chief of Police's shack, across the Line, faced toward the railroad, guns in their hands. Everything got very quiet again. The flies buzzed. Voices sounded from the distance. But no one rushed down the street where Gruttel was lying.

"Lucky devil!" Ben said slowly. "He went out quick!"

I swore softly. "How about the century you handed him? Do we go down and get it?"

Ben Breed smiled grimly. "I never try to pass bum money, Mac," he stated. "Knew he wouldn't get far. The Wop gave him a job—and he did it."

I stared at Ben. His gray eyes were narrowed on the body sprawled face downward, a block away. A few Mexicans were approaching it slowly. Some ragged kids ran up. My eyes went to the shuttered windows of the shacks lining the street in which Gruttel had died.

"You mean—" I said slowly—"that the Wop sent him to us, with a fake yarn about the Bisbee job?"

Ben shook his head. "The Wop knew I'd been working on Gruttel for a squeal—that's what I mean, Mac," he said slowly, his voice soft and hoarse. "When Gruttel told him he was breaking, before Bugs came in—the Wop let him go."

"How'd he know you were working on Gruttel?" I asked slowly.

"I saw that he *did* know," Ben returned quietly. "Squarehead was wanted for murder, anyway. I saved the State some trouble."

I grunted. "All right. But what did you get out of it? You got Gruttel bumped out of things. You slipped him a counterfeit century note for something you knew was no good—before he handed it to you."

Ben Breed stretched himself out on the bed. There was a crowd around Gruttel's body. I turned away from the window.

"Mac—" Ben's voice was almost cheerful—"you don't wise up to this Mex baby. He's tricky. Maybe he figures I'll be as dumb as you. Maybe he figures I'll rate that Bisbee stuff as all wet. Just something he gave Gruttel to spill for me."

I stared. Ben picked himself out a black pill. He lighted it. His fingers were as steady as those of a stud poker dealer at Tia Juana's Foreign Club. He smiled with his lips.

"But I don't rate it that way, Mac. We stick inside this room for an hour or so. Then we go out and climb into the crate. We wing it for Tia Juana. It'll be dark before we take off from the spot where I set the ship down. We circle around to the north—and then fly eastward. Somewhere between Tombstone and Bisbee we hit sand and mesquite again. We make ourselves look different—and go up Mule Mountain. The Wop needs coin to fight Cards Ganlin. The Bisbee bank is just one that'll have it waiting for him."

I stared at Ben Breed. The Wop figured that Ben would fly

for some other town, if he gave Gruttel the Bisbee story to spill. That was the way Ben guessed the Wop was figuring. But maybe he was guessing wrong.

"Gruttel may have faked up that story," I stated. "Maybe it didn't come from the Wop."

Ben grunted. "They didn't bump him off until *after* he'd been up to see us," he said quietly.

That was true enough. I lighted a pill. Ben was lying with his eyes closed, his lean face was expressionless.

"Just the two of us going in on this, Ben?" I asked slowly.

He nodded. "There's only *one* Antonio Flores," he replied slowly. "To hell with the bank. We want the Wop. If we get him—the Border gang's smashed right. Before or after the stick-up—it's all the same."

"That's a tough spot," I muttered, thinking of Bisbee and Mule Mountain—the narrow pass, sloping mountain earth on both sides of the copper town. "I've got a hunch the Wop's not pulling anything there."

Ben Breed yawned. He did it noisily. His gray eyes met mine—he smiled grimly.

"The killing's been done in low country, Mac," he said slowly. "Around Douglas, Agua Prieta and Tia Juana. Flores is an expert. He likes variety. Bisbee is up in the air a bit. High death—that's *my* hunch. And I'm playing it all the way."

I swore. "We can loaf around up there—and read all about the Wop pulling a job around El Paso, or right in this section," I stated slowly.

Ben Breed was breathing evenly. I stared over at him. His whole body was relaxed.

"That pass is a bad place to get out of," I muttered. "Even if they pulled the job sweet-like—"

I stopped. There wasn't much use going on. Ben was sound asleep.

THE TWO-SEATER BANKED around at fifty degrees. It was a moonlight night; the air was very calm. Ben had been flying from the front cockpit, winging us around in a circle. In the sky ahead was a glare of white light. It was reflected light— streaking up from the copper town of Bisbee. Mule Mountain rose blackly from the semi-desert stretches to the north of town. Ben spoke through the phone-set strapped over his helmet, his voice coming to me above the roar of the engine.

"We'll cut the running lights—glide for it. The road below is the one running up through town. Watch to the left of it for a landing place. I'll take the right side. Mesquite won't bother us so much, but look out for cacti—that'll rip us badly."

The roar of the engine died abruptly. The running lights on the wings blinked out. We had been flying at seven thousand— the ship was in a mild dive now. Ben was holding her glide-path parallel to the winding road below. Already the earth was sloping up toward the crest of the pass through Bisbee. Behind and slightly to the northward was Tombstone. To the south, down along the Border, were the towns of Douglas and Agua Prieta. Lights from Douglas flared in the sky—the Mexican town was almost dark.

It was ten minutes after eleven by my wrist-watch. We had left Mexicali more than five hours ago, before it was dark—and had flown out toward Tia Juana. Then we had circled around, beyond sight of Mexicali, winging back to the north of the

Border. Now we were nearing Bisbee—and gliding without lights or exhaust roar for a landing spot.

There was only the faint shrill of wind through the wires and struts of the two-seater. I stared over the side of the fuselage, to the left of the road below. There was no traffic on the road. Boulders and mesquite dotted the rugged country; I saw no spot cleared enough to set the ship down.

"All right, Mac!" Ben's voice came to me through the phone-set. "Got a stretch over here—we'll stall down. Maybe catch a ride up to town. Looks good enough to—"

He stopped talking. Above the shrill of the wind through the ship's rigging I heard another sound—a new sound. The roar of a plane's engine!

Jerking my head to the right—I saw her. She carried no running lights. The trail of her exhaust slanted up into the sky behind her. That meant that the ship was diving. Her outline was not too clear in the night sky—but she was winging toward our ship, and from the direction of Bisbee!

"Swing that Browning!" Ben's voice was cool; the hoarseness was gone now. "I'll bank away from her. If she comes at us—don't wait—too long!"

I swung the bracketed machine-gun, stripping off the canvas covering. She was loaded for action, well oiled. The other plane was diving at us from an angle. She changed her course as Ben banked off to the left, half circled the ship. I glanced at the altimeter. We were down to five thousand feet.

"They've pulled the job!" I muttered through the phone-set mouthpiece. "We blunder into the get-away ship and they think—"

"Watch 'em!" Ben cut in. "They haven't pulled anything—not yet!"

The ship was streaking down at us as Ben came around—leveled off from the bank. She was within an eighth of a mile now. I caught the gleam of a machine-gun. She was a single-seater. Now she was fifty yards distant. Ben banked slightly. My right forefinger tightened on the trigger of the Browning. I cramped the third finger against the trigger—for a sure pull.

The steam-rivet clatter of the single-seater's machine-gun sounded. Red streaked down at us—below us. I thought for a split second that the landing gear was gone. And then the single-seater was zooming. And as she zoomed I squeezed the trigger of the Browning. She was close—and the shot was perfect.

I could almost see the bullets tearing up through her under-gear, ripping up through the floor of the tiny cockpit. I held fire for a long burst—and then Ben was banking around.

"You—got her!" His voice sounded choked. "My bus—Mac!"

She was going down in a tight spin. Flames streaked up from her as she dove. I was stiff in the cockpit. Ben Breed's bus—the one the Wop had stolen outside of Douglas! And that meant—

"We got Flores, Ben!" My voice was pitched high. "That's the finish of—"

"Like hell we got him!" Ben's voice cut in on mine. "They spotted us—"

He broke off, nosing the ship down again. There was a flash of red, a rising ball of flame, from the rock and mesquite to the left of the road. The death crash of the single-seater came up to us.

We circled—and then the engine of the two-seater roared again. Ben twisted his head.

"Got to—change plans!" he muttered. "We'll get in closer.

That wasn't the Wop flying that ship. He's too damn good to go down like that—"

He jerked his head to the front again. Mechanically I got the canvas cover over the Browning. There was no other exhaust color in the sky. Below, back of us now, was the flaming wreckage of the single-seater. Not the Wop—flying her? And yet—she had been the Wop's plane. That meant that Ben had guessed right. Flores and his gang were close to Bisbee, if not already in the town.

"Got to get clear—of the wreckage!" Ben's voice sounded through the receivers fixed over my ears. "We'll take a chance—pick a spot up on the slope."

"Might have been the Wop—flying that ship," I insisted. "Maybe we should drop down—"

"Nothing doing!" Ben's voice was steady, sharp. "They spotted us—someone saw us circle, buzzed one of the gang. Afraid of that. We got too close to Tucson, coming up."

I swore softly. It wasn't at all improbable that some of the Wop's men had spotted us. We hadn't showed at Tia Juana. The Wop had men there. And yet—what could two of us do against the gang?

I smiled grimly. It wasn't two of us, I knew that. It was Breed that Flores feared. Ben Breed. The lean-faced, stoop-shouldered gent who was winging the two-seater up toward the crest of the Mule Mountain pass. Twice in the past month Ben had taken lickings from the Border gang. Twice had the Wop got clear of us. But each time the gang had suffered. Each time the Wop had reason to use all of his cleverness, to fight desperately in order to get in the clear.

"High death!" I muttered grimly, thinking of Ben's words in

the heated room back at the Red House. "It was almost that for us—minutes ago. And they know we're coming in. They'll be on the lookout for us—now."

The two-seater was gliding. Ben's head was over the right side of the fuselage. The road was of white, crushed rock. It stood out in the moonlight. The grade was steep at this point; the road curved sharply. Boulders and mesquite rimmed it—below. But to the right of the curve, beyond the boulders, was a level stretch. It was narrow—fairly long. The ship was over in a ninety-degree bank—she started to slip off on a wing.

For a thousand feet she slipped—and then Ben pulled her out of it. He glided for the narrow stretch. There was a wind in the pass; it made the landing tricky. Fifty feet above the stretch—and Ben was pulling the stick back—the nose of the two-seater was coming up. He was stalling for the landing.

She was ten feet off the earth when she lost all forward speed. Her nose was slanted upward, at an angle of about thirty degrees. She started to drop, like an elevator, only the weight of the engine whipped the nose down faster than the tail assembly. She struck heavily—but in a pan-cake landing. There was the crackling of landing-gear, but the wings held. I rocked in the rear cockpit, my body relaxed for the shock. And then I was snapping the safety-belt buckle, was climbing down from the cockpit. Ben snapped the engine switch, climbed down from the front cockpit. He dropped to his knees, inspected the landing gear. I glanced back in the direction of the crashed plane. There was a faint glare of red in the sky above the spot.

Ben Breed straightened up. He spoke grimly.

"We're here—but we won't get off in a hurry. Not unless we run into some spare parts up in—"

He stopped. I was grinning. "We may run into something," I stated, "but it won't be spare parts. What next?"

Ben jerked off his helmet and goggles. He walked around a bit, getting the cramps out of his legs. I did the same. Ben spoke.

"We'll go in as a couple of bums," he stated. "Get that make-up box out of the rear cockpit. The ship's pretty well concealed. Maybe we can bum a ride up to town—maybe not. Can't be more than five or six miles."

I nodded—got the black box from the rear cockpit. There was a flashlight under the seat. I took it along to Ben.

"Get some dirt—smear it on your face," he ordered. "That oil kicked back from the engine will help the job. Rip that shirt of yours a bit. How'd you like a patch over your left eye?"

I shook my head. "Anything—but that," I returned. "I want two good eyes on this job."

Ben Breed grinned. "You'll need 'em!" he stated. "You can pick up a limp, instead."

"That's better," I replied. "I don't have to sight a Colt with my leg."

A HALF HOUR later we hit the road that climbed toward Bisbee. Two cars passed us, a mile from the spot where Ben had set the two-seater down. Neither of them stopped. One was a battered flivver that was having a lot of trouble making the grade—the other was a big, closed car, traveling fast and with the curtains down. We kept moving.

Houses, mine shacks commenced to spring up on both sides of the road. It ceased to be dirt, became very rough macadam. The air was clear—and cool. It was blowing a bit. The road curved continually. It was pretty tough walking. We plodded on, and finally we reached a fairly straight stretch. Street lights were hung across the road from poles—there were shacks on both sides. The mountain rose blackly from the pass; we could see lights gleaming in houses on both sides.

"Pick up the limp," Ben muttered. "And hold it—from now until—"

We were approaching a gas station. A roadster coming up the pass pulled in. The driver climbed down. He called loudly for some guy named "Jake." It was a cinch that he was excited. I limped along beside Ben. We were both ragged, dirty. Ben hadn't used much make-up on my face—but he'd worked for a half hour on his. He looked old, was wearing a scraggly, gray wig.

A chap shoved his head out of a raised window, above the front of the gas station.

"What in hell's the matter?" He yelled. "I'm not selling gas at this—"

"It ain't gas." The one who had yelled from below cut in. "An aeroplane fell—down by Red Flats. Smashed all to hell."

Ben pulled me over to one side of the road. We stopped, listened. The bird in the window was a cool one.

"Yeah?" he came back. "Anyone hurt?"

The one who had climbed down from the ancient roadster swore.

"Chuck Free was ridin' her," he stated. "He was smashed to pieces."

I stared at Ben. There was a frown on his face. The fellow in the window swore softly. He shook his head from side to side.

"Get hold of Johnny Roon, up at the High Spot," he

instructed, and I noticed that his voice dropped considerably. "Tell him what happened. Got me?"

"Sure," the man below replied. "There was another ship in the sky—when Chuck went down. He an' the other guy spilled lead."

The man in the window swore again. "Get Roon—tell it to him," he repeated, and slammed the window down.

The roadster was driven off. Ben gripped me by the arm. His voice was hard.

"We get a break here," he muttered. "Let's move fast."

"Who in hell's Chuck Free?" I whispered. "And how come he tackles us without any hesitation?"

Ben was moving along the road. I followed, limping. The road wasn't getting any wider, but it was getting more populated. We did a half mile before Ben answered one of my questions.

"That bird tackled us because he knew we were coming in. That means the Wop knew it, too. He'll know that we're *in*, now. That makes it tougher. There's just one thing for the Wop to do—now. Pull the bank job in a hurry. Just after she opens up tomorrow. He can't afford to wait. He'll be afraid we'll buzz the wires. Knows we didn't fall for his Gruttel bluff. He'll pull the job in a rush—or run out on us."

I grunted. "No landing gear to lift us off—on our crate," I reminded him. "We can't get out—*that* way."

"We get *in*—first," Ben stated slowly. "We're looking for the High Spot—and one Johnny Roon. It'll be sort of mutual—ten to one Johnny'll be looking for us."

I smiled grimly, limping along the road beside Ben. His long arms were swinging loosely at his side. He walked with a shuffle now. I stressed my limp a bit. We were getting into town.

Houses and shacks on the sides of the mountain, above the road that followed the pass.

"No bet, Ben," I returned, keeping clear of the right tag. "You're too good for me. I'm beginning to think something's on, at that."

Ben swore softly. "We got until bank opening time to find out the details," he stated in a low voice. "We'll play it alone—the bulls up here might ball things up. They might treat the Wop like a common killer."

I smiled with tight lips. There was no danger of us doing that little thing. Two plays—the Wop had made since Cards Ganlin had chased him out of Tia Juana. He had used Gruttel, failed—and had killed. He had used another gent—and that pilot was out of the game. But things were tight—and getting tighter.

A short individual was moving toward us, on our side of the road. He was unsteady on his feet. Ben watched him closely. He was beside us before Breed spoke.

"Lookin' for the High Spot, Buddy—Chuck Free told us a couple of days back—might be a hand-out—"

I stiffened. Ben was working so fast he caught me sleeping. The short individual straightened. He stopped swaying. I got a look at his eyes. They were dark, slitted.

"Yeah?" he breathed, very slowly. "You go down the road an' turn—"

He wore a sheepskin coat, and the right pocket moved just a bit. I saw that—and Ben saw it, too. From the left pocket of his own ragged coat there sounded a pop-cough. Something cracked sharply. Ben sucked in his breath, stiffened. The short man cried out hoarsely—took a step forward. Ben caught him in his arms as he slumped. His left hand hung at his side.

"Get this guy—over in the stuff—"

I dragged the short bird to the growth at one side of the road. There were some houses up the grade a bit. A window slammed. My right hand touched the skin over the short man's heart. He was done. I rolled him face downward, turned back toward Ben. He was holding his left hand above the wrist. Red trailed over his fingers.

"Come on!" he muttered. "Did you—spot him?"

I shook my head. "You got him with your left, Ben!" I muttered. "Did he hit you on the bone? Flesh wound or—"

"Ripped off some skin." Ben led the way up a narrow path on the opposite side of the road. "Bunny Freel, that was. Funny. Used to be with Ganlin. He spotted me—had to let her go. Had a finger on steel—"

Voices sounded down along the road. We were up the side of the mountain a few hundred yards. Ben dropped down.

"Got a handkerchief?" he muttered. "Get her tied around my wrist. Nothing bad. Had a finger on each gun, Mac—never would have hit him with the left, only we were right on top of each other. Thought I could stop his shot—kill the noise. That's off now. The Wop'll know we're in. May be too late—"

Low bushes fringed the trail. I got a look at Ben's wrist. The skin was ripped, no arteries smashed. No powder burns—they hadn't been that close. I used two handkerchiefs in a tight job of bandaging.

"How in hell did he spot you, Ben?" I whispered. "With that make-up—"

Ben grunted. "It's no good, Mac," he came back. "They know

my size. They know there's two of us—and they know we're coming in. I bluffed on Free. It didn't work. I could tell by the way he talked that he was set for a kill. Didn't get him soon enough—"

Voices sounded from below. Then suddenly they died. Ben got his mouth close to my right ear.

"Found him—get moving. Don't talk."

He led the way up the side of the mountain. The trail widened. It was joined by another. It ran along the side of the mountain, without climbing, for perhaps a quarter mile. Then it started to climb again. Moonlight filtered down through stubby trees. Above there was rocky soil—mesquite. A battered sign lay just off the trail. Ben halted, pointed toward it. I stared down.

" 'High Spot'!" I muttered. "Where in hell—"

"Up above," Ben whispered. "Not far. Miners' gambling shack. Run by a bird named Charlie Brenner. Remember her now—she used to be called 'Charlie's Perch.' Tagged on a new name. Came up here once, after a guy."

I nodded. There weren't many spots in the Border towns, or the near-Border towns, that Ben Breed hadn't visited at one time or another.

"Do we go up?" I muttered.

Ben nodded his head. "The Wop knows about Free—not about Bunny. If he's up above—"

He wasn't. We spent twenty minutes looking over the slope around the house. Another ten getting up close. The place was dark. The doors and windows were barricaded. Things looked as if the place hadn't been used for months. We sat on the back steps, with the mountain looming up in front of us, and

I rebandaged Ben's wound. It wasn't much—just a lot of skin mussed up. There was a stream running down near the place, and I washed it out.

We smoked a couple of pills. I looked at my wrist-watch, which I was carrying in a pocket. It was twenty minutes after one. We'd come up the slope slowly—she was a stiff one. Ben was sitting with his eyes half closed. I could see that he was thinking.

"Mac," he said slowly, "we're licked. We can't get to 'em. My guess is that they're cutting off the road—they've got a lot of men up here. They know we're in. I'd give a lot to grab off the Wop—but it won't work. Not this trip. We'll play it—the other way."

I stared at him. He smiled grimly.

"We'll get to a phone—call the bank officials, the police. We'll spill the deal—give them a chance to save the coin. It's the best bet."

I grunted. "Even that's no cinch," I stated. "We've got to *get* to the phone."

Ben stood up. His face was twisted; he looked sort of old.

"Worth a try," he stated slowly. "We'll split. B. Coley's the president. A guy named Jason's the cashier. There's a little runt named Goddard, a pretty wise bird, who handles the bulls up here. We'll go into town. I'll head for a phone. If I don't make it—you finish the deal. Trail me—I'll go slow. If I do make it—trail me some more. We'll sit in for the attempt."

"Won't be any," I said slowly. "The Wop'll know the call went through. They won't try for the coin—but they may try for us."

Ben smiled with his lips. "That's *one* way of figuring it," he stated slowly. "Just one. Let's go!"

THE TOWN WAS quiet. There was an eating place with some white lights inside. I stepped into the doorway of a closed drugstore, lighted a pill. A bus roared through the town, exhausts making a lot of racket. It didn't stop. Ben Breed was moving slowly toward the eating place—and a telephone. I swore harshly. It was a tough spot. If we spoiled this deal for the Wop—we were on the circle for a kill. That much was certain.

I puffed at the cigarette—watched Ben move toward the entrance of the eating place. I glanced up the street, across it. A fairly modern building caught my eyes. It was painted white, or perhaps it was of white-washed brick. The windows were barred—and I caught three letters on one of them— "ANK." The street lights didn't hit the others.

This wasn't the center of town. I stared toward the white building. It was a one-story affair.

"Bank," I muttered. "Might be the one—"

I stopped muttering. Two men came running out from the entrance. They kept right on running. One turned to the right, the other to the left. My ears picked up a faint drone, from skyward. I commenced to tingle inside. And then, suddenly, I stopped tingling. I shook.

And everything else shook. There was one deafening roar. Glass clattered. Nothing happened to the front of the bank— but there was a cloud of dirt and dust hurled into the air, at the rear. The man who had run to the left was bent low. He whirled around, ran back toward the bank. Two men came running from the right. They headed for the main entrance, vanished from sight.

And then things commenced to happen. Two cars pulled into sight. They came up fast—and both pulled up on the sidewalk, in front of the bank. Men spilled out of them—eight or ten humans. They had two machine-guns—and they set them up in the center of the road. Most of the men had rifles.

A figure ran out from the eating place, shouting wildly. One of the men who had come up in the first car raised his rifle. It cracked. The shouting man sprawled in the middle of the street.

Two men came running up from the center of town. One of the machine-guns started a staccato clatter. From the distance there came the echo of two shots. I got back in the entrance of the closed drugstore. The bust was on—and it was on right!

The irony of the thing was that Ben was in the eating place, trying to phone out a warning. And the job was about done. Well placed dynamite—a sweet organization—

Some more shots sounded, from the distance. That was easy to figure. Some of the gang were stopping curious folk from getting along the road. Or maybe just keeping it cleared—for the get-away. It was my guess that the two cars would take out the coin in the direction in which they were headed, which was southward. That would give the Wop a chance to make the Border at Agua Prieta, or some spot near that place.

Voices sounded from the rear of the bank. Smoke was rising, but not much of it. I heard the sizzling of something that sounded like a fire extinguisher. The Wop was after big coin—he had dug for it—with high explosive.

I swore grimly. Then I heard the drone again. It died abruptly. Two men came plunging down a narrow street, down the mountain-side. One of them took a rifle bullet before he knew what it was all about. The other started to run toward my hide-out. He didn't make it.

Machine-gun lead stopped him. Bullets ricocheted off the wood of the store front, below the glass level. The man who had run for shelter flattened out in the street, near the curb. There was a lull in the shooting—and a shrill whistling reached my ears. I raised my head a bit—stared upward. Coming down in a stall landing was a plane!

Then I got it. Got the reason for the two cars pulling up on the sidewalk, off the street. I thought of our ship—and the smashed landing gear. No worry for the Wop—no worry about getting down the mountain grades, about being intercepted by wire. The street was wide enough. And smooth enough. With the coin in the ship—

The knob on the door, back of me, rattled. I swung about. My Colt was in my right hand. Through the glass I saw a face—the face of Antonio Flores! The Wop!

I raised the gun, started to squeeze the trigger. Glass wouldn't deflect the forty-five's lead—not enough to do any harm. The range was too close.

But I didn't squeeze the trigger. The Wop's hands were raised and empty. Both of them. A voice came to me, faintly.

"Easy, Mac—I'll open her!"

Ben Breed's voice! Ben Breed—back of the Wop—holding a gun on him! The lock clicked. The door opened, inward.

"Inside!" Ben's voice was harsh. "Make it fast, Mac—and close the door!"

I did both. Faint light from the street reached the interior of the store. It was small—and smelled of cheap candy. I got a look at the Wop's face. It was pasty white. Ben loomed more than a foot taller than the short, thick-set half breed. The muscles of Flores' mouth twitched. His hands were held above his shoulders—Ben held his Maxim-silenced pistol high, in his right hand.

"They blew her wide, Ben!" I spoke grimly. "Ship coming down—for the fly out!"

Breed stiffened. "Plane?" he muttered. "Where in hell can they land—"

"She's landing now!" I cut in. "In the street—"

"Fifty grand, on the spot—if you ease me out!" The Wop spoke thickly, hoarsely. His eyes were on Breed's.

Ben swore. "You're worth more than that—dead!" he snapped.

The Wop's black eyes narrowed. He was swaying from side to side. More shots sounded from the street.

"Cut that stuff!" Ben's voice was like ice, sharper than the sight on his thirty-eight. "Stand still!"

The Wop stiffened. Ben backed off from him. The roar of a ship's engine sounded again. I cried out.

"She didn't come down—not that time?"

Ben was smiling with tight-pressed lips, smiling into the narrowed eyes of the Wop.

"She won't come down!" he stated harshly. "There's tricky wind up there—she'll never make the glide in."

The Wop sucked in his breath sharply. Voices sounded from outside, raised hoarsely. The roar of the engine died again.

"Heard the explosion—went out the back of the eat house." Ben's voice held an amused note. "Damned if I didn't stumble into the Wop—he was shooting off a signal light—giving that pilot direction. Why didn't you fly the ship yourself, Wop? Yellow?"

Flores cursed fiercely. Ben spoke again.

"They won't get down the mountain with the stuff, Flores.

That blow-up raised hell with their chances—but not with yours, eh?"

I stared at Ben. He was smiling. A machine-gun clattered again.

"Can't we do something?" I was thinking of the scrap outside, the coin.

Ben spoke sharply. "We're doing plenty! We'll wait till the boys outside gather up their playthings off the street," he snapped. "Want to go out and get yourself sprayed? Even the Wop wouldn't do that. Wouldn't risk setting the ship down. But he *would* take it off, eh, Flores?"

The Wop spoke thickly. "Hundred grand! Let me loose!"

Ben Breed swore. "Playing it safe!" he sneered. "Cards scared the guts out of him, Mac. Shows yellow all the way. If that pilot sets that little ship down right—the Wop plans to fly out the coin. If he crashes—Flores rides down with the boys."

The engine of the plane circling over the street sounded again. Ben's eyes never left those of Antonio Flores.

"We've got 'em this time, Mac!" he stated grimly. "Without the Wop—they haven't a chance, even if they do get down the mountain-side. They'll kill each other off—for the coin. Cards even worked one of his men in the gang—Bunny Freel. They'll shoot it out—"

"You lie!" The Wop's voice was hoarse. "I bought Bunny—"

There was the scream of a plane's wires— the exhaust roar had died again. Voices shouted wildly—beyond the store, in the street. The Wop raised his head. The wire shrill was louder. There was the sudden roar of the engine—

And then the roof of the drugstore seemed suddenly to shatter. There was a screaming crash. Wood crackled, glass within the store was shattered from the shelves. I saw the Wop pitch to one side, shouted hoarsely—

"The plane—shoot!"

It seemed to me that Ben Breed's gun pop-coughed—I couldn't be sure. Only one fact was clear, in the split second before something pounded on the side of my head and sent me down into a sea of blackness. And that fact was that the plane had crashed through the roof of the one-story building. The money would never go out by air.

WHEN I CAME out of it I was lying on a cot. The room was quiet.

I turned my head slowly, and Ben Breed grinned down at me. His left arm was in a sling. He looked white and tired. I started to speak, but he stopped me.

"Detailed report," he stated. "Pilot of the plane was killed. Not identified. Three of the gang killed—only one identified. Four citizens hurt, one killed. No money taken from the bank—"

"No money—" I struggled to sit up, but a wave of dizziness sent me down again.

"None in the vault," Ben said slowly. "Payroll coin transfer date changed. Coming up tomorrow. Officials decided to change it—for safety. Great idea."

I blinked. Ben frowned. "The Wop's among those not present," he stated quietly.

"You got him?" I muttered.

Ben shook his head. "Stuff from the roof slammed me down. Got my left arm and shoulder. Missed Flores on the first shot—after that I didn't see him. He dived for the counter—

and that piece of furniture must have held the wreckage of the roof away from him. I was pinned down—finally dragged you out. The two cars made the try—southward. One of 'em turned over on a grade. The other got clear. Maybe the Wop was in it—maybe not."

I groaned. Ben grinned. "You got a bump on the head—no fracture. Too tough, in a few days you'll be up."

I thought that one over. "What then?" I asked slowly.

Ben Breed's face twisted. The grin faded. But he got part of it back again, before he answered that one.

"I'm riding the Wop's tail!" he stated. "It's tough riding—and the breaks aren't so good. We didn't get much out of this deal. But neither did Flores. Sticking?"

I swore slowly. Ben Breed nodded. He lighted a pill for me, then one for himself.

"Figured you would," he said quietly. "We'll keep on shoving out the chips—the Wop's hand wasn't so good this time. He played 'em high—and the elevation helped to lick him. But even if the ship *had* come down—"

Ben shrugged his shoulders. He pulled on his cigarette.

"High death!" he muttered slowly. "A lot of us got close to it—this time."

Red Wings

Antonio Flores, the fighting, flying bandit leader, puts over a fast one on Ben Breed, the Federal op, and Mac, the ex-flier. A battle on the ground and a battle in the air.

THE RED STREET car clattered over the bridge. It was very hot, and the odors in the car were not so good. I sat between a fat Mexican woman with two kids on her ample lap—and an ancient Mex gent whose breath was a combination of *tequila* and any number of warm, native dishes. There wasn't much water in the Rio Grande, and the mud produced another odor.

The car reached the Juarez side of the river, and the Inspectors boarded her. I lifted my El Paso paper, and watched the little Mex seated across from me. He seemed very sleepy; his small, black eyes were almost closed. But he wasn't sleepy. He'd been tagging me around El Paso for more than an hour, and now he was riding across the Border with me. I was interested.

The Inspector lowered my paper and stared at me. His face was expressionless. He moved on up the car. He poked in the bag a Mex woman held on her lap, muttered to himself, and dropped off the front end of the car, I raised my paper again. The insignificant Mex had his lids almost closed as I glanced over the top of the sheet. He had a pock-marked face and a black, drooping mustache; wore a soiled lightweight suit and a battered hat.

The American Inspector came through the car. He paid little attention to the Mexican passengers, and not so much to the Americans. He dropped off the front step—the car got into motion jerkily. I lowered my paper, jumped to my feet, took three steps toward the front platform of the car. Then I

twisted my head. The little Mex was stiff in his seat—his dark eyes were wide.

I stared out of the window behind him, swore softly, went back to the seat and dropped down. I didn't smile. The Mex closed his eyes again. I wasn't suspicious of him now. Not at all—I was *sure*. My little faked break for the platform had shown me that I was his man.

It was around five o'clock. Ben Breed had left me three hours before—and had told me to meet him at *El Pajaro's* place, at five-thirty. I'd started early. And, even so, it looked as though I might be late arriving. One thing was sure—the pock-marked Mex wouldn't be trailing me when I went into the 'dobe shack three blocks off the Juarez main street. Not to "the Bird's" place. Not with Breed inside, and with something important on.

The street car rattled southward for about four blocks. Then it turned to the west. Main street. About five blocks in this direction—then it would turn northward, cross the river again. At the third block I got up, went to the platform, dropped off.

I angled up to a Mex cigar stand and bought myself two

packs of *Elegantes*. While I was lighting one, I glanced around. The pock-marked one wasn't in sight. The street car in which I had been transported across the mud and shallow water rattled past the cigar stand. The crowd behind me had held it up. I was on the right side for a glance at the seat my Mex friend *had* occupied. The tense is correct. He wasn't among those present.

In the rear of the cigar stand there was a bar. I went back and had some *cerveza*. It was green beer, but it was cold. The Mex didn't show. I went further back, looking for an alley. It wasn't hard to find. I turned westward, and strolled along. *El Pajaro's* place was five minutes' walk—if I'd lost my Mex. And it looked that way.

I had my back turned to the street into which the alley led—when I heard some one choking. It was the sort of a choke a human lets out when a knife slides into his back, between the ribs. I swung around—and slid my right hand into the right pocket of my light suit.

A figure came out into the alley. It was the figure of the pock-marked one—and he was sick. He emerged from the rear of a shack in the direction in which I had been headed. It looked like just another bar and beer shack.

The Mex didn't pay any attention to me. He had one hand behind his back. His knees buckled and he collapsed in the dirt of the alley. He coughed a couple more times—and then ceased to move. I got behind a pile of a half dozen kegs—and waited. Nothing happened. Five minutes passed. I went out and looked the Mex over. He was finished with riding across the Rio on the El Paso-Juarez street car. I didn't pull the knife out of his back. It had a long handle—and very probably a longer blade.

I fished in a pocket of his soiled suit and got loose an envelope. It was dirty—but there was a drawing on it. The drawing looked interesting. I shoved the envelope in my pocket—and listened to a couple of voices. They got louder. It was time to move.

Five minutes later I was sipping a beer in the *Red Rose*, and staring at the drawing on one side of the envelope. It was a pretty fair sketch of a plane—in flight. The plane was a single-seater with a round fuselage. The wings were done in red. For a couple of seconds I got the idea that the red was ink. I stuck a finger in some of the beer I didn't intend to drink—and touched the red. It had a peculiar quality. It didn't look so much like ink—and it felt different.

I paid for the beer, stuck the envelope in my pocket, and headed for *El Pajaro's* place. There was something I wanted Ben Breed to tell me. Five days had passed since the Wop had got clear, up in Bisbee. A pock-marked Mex had trailed me all over El Paso. He'd ridden across the Line with me. I'd ducked him for a few seconds—and someone had stuck a knife in his back. That was cute—but it was the sketch on the envelope that got me. Perhaps Breed could make a guess on that. The ship looked a lot like the one the Wop had stolen from him, down in Douglas. It had a round fuselage. But it had red wings. And they hadn't been drawn with ink. Maybe Ben Breed could tell me why a Mex was trailing me, with a ship sketch in his pocket, and with the wings done in—blood!

EL PAJARO'S PLACE looked a lot like a stable, and it smelled exactly like one. The owner of this 'dobe shack was a runt of a Mex with thick lips and his left arm absent from his squat body. He loved to whistle—and he could imitate all sorts of Mexican birds. Thus the tag. I went into the semi-darkness of the shack, blinked a few times, and headed for the back room.

There didn't seem to be anyone around. There were rough planks on the floor, and you had to take a step down to get into the little room where I was to meet Ben Breed. I took the step—but not down. My right foot touched something that was soft—and felt human. I stepped back, got my Colt out of my pocket and backed into the other room. I bent over and called out in a low tone.

"Breed!"

Silence. There wasn't even the heavy breathing of a drunk. Something was wrong. I moved up toward the little room again. I listened for several minutes. Then I struck a match, holding it at arm's length, and keeping my body to one side. I stared down at the motionless figure.

It wasn't Ben Breed. It was *El Pajaro*. There was a small, dark red spot just over his right eye. I felt his right wrist. He hadn't been dead very long. There was a rough table in the little room, and last night there had been a lamp on it. I fumbled around, found the table and the lamp. It lighted up. There wasn't much in the place to be mussed up—but the little that there was hadn't been touched. There were three chairs—not one overturned. I looked at the table. A pack of black-papered cigarettes rested on end. Ben Breed's brand.

I shivered a bit. Then, suddenly, there was a whistle. It stiffened me—the sound of it. I'd heard *El Pajaro* whistle and this shrilling was the same thing. Crouching back of the table, I held the Colt ready for action—and waited. The whistle sounded again—then there was a lot of silence.

Then, very close, I heard breath sucked in sharply. A shape edged into the outside rim of lamp light. A tall, skinny shape—slightly stooped. Ben Breed!

He was staring down at the figure of the Mexican who had once been a good imitator of birds. He didn't bend over. His eyes were on the lighted lamp. I straightened up, spoke grimly.

"Hello, Ben! Small calibre bullet through the Bird's head. Gave me a jolt when I came in. No light—thought it was—"

I stopped. Ben Breed spoke in his husky voice. It was little more than a whisper.

"Happened ten minutes ago," he stated. "Cards Ganlin's on this side. He was trailing me. Thought I shook him off—came in here. Two greasers followed me in. I didn't like their looks, got back of the bar. Didn't know where *El Pajaro* was—so I played his stuff. Whistled, bent over back of the bar. The next thing I knew there was a crack—and the two Mex were outside. This poor devil was down—and finished."

I nodded. "Why in hell—" I muttered "—would Cards want you? If they were his men—"

Ben Breed cut in. "Didn't say they *were* his men," he stated. "I said he was on this side of the Rio, that's all."

I stared down at *El Pajaro's* body. "Someone figured you got yours," I muttered, "That whistle of yours—"

"Gave *El Pajaro* the lead meant for me!" Ben cut in, and there was bitterness in his tone. "Mac—I've got a hunch the Wop Flores is across the river."

I nodded. Reaching into my pocket, I pulled out the soiled envelope. Breed moved up to the table and the light of the lamp. His gray eyes narrowed as he saw the sketch. I told him the story.

"That red stuff isn't ink," I finished. "It's blood."

Ben Breed took a black-papered cigarette from the up-ended pack and lighted it. He looked the sketch over carefully.

"Maybe it is—maybe not," he stated. "I know a fellow across the Rio that's something of a chemist. Not that it matters much—she's my rotary-engined ship. This Mex who carried the envelope—he was trailing you. My guess is that he wanted to get this to me."

"Why?" I snapped grimly.

Breed swore. His voice was low, husky in tone. He smiled with his lips.

"Mac—" he said slowly—"the Wop and Cards Ganlin— they're fighting it to the finish. They both know how we stand. We're after the Wop. They know we're in it to the finish, too. It means a lot to you—to get Flores. It's part of my job—to keep the Border clear of his brand of human. We're in it deep, Mac—and Ganlin knows it. If he had information that would help us—he'd see that we got it. And the Wop would see that we *didn't*—"

I swore softly. "The sketch of that ship—"

Ben Breed's eyes were narrowed to little slits. He spoke tone-lessly.

"That Mex trailing you—maybe he'd been told something, but not too much. Someone gave him this sketch. It's a draw-ing of my old ship. If my hunch is right, and the Wop's in town—he flew in!"

I nodded. "But why the red wings?" I asked slowly. "That ship of yours is painted gray—"

Ben Breed smiled grimly. "A knife in the back—for a Mex that has something that wouldn't hurt us any to look at," he breathed. "And a bullet in the head for a Mex that someone thought was me. The Wop's around, Mac. And so is Ganlin."

I shook my head slowly. "Flores has got your single-seater," I stated. "She's fast—and she mounts a Browning. All we've got is that battered D.H. two-seater, with the bracketed Lewis-gun. We've got to keep out of the air, Ben."

Breed straightened. "The Wop's licked us twice, Mac—" he said slowly—"and he got a draw the other time. We're spoiling his chances to get coin. Each time we spoil—he gets more desperate. And Cards is fighting him hard. The two greasers that got *El Pajaro*—and thought they got me—they'll give Flores the news. Ten to one they're his men. But the Wop knows his stuff—he'll want a look-see. He isn't so far away. He'll—"

"Come here!" I finished grimly. "If he does—"

Ben Breed cut in sharply. "If he does—we'll have our hands full!" he stated. "He won't blunder in. Now listen—"

He spoke slowly, expressionlessly—and I listened. From somewhere along the narrow street came the sound of a squeaky phonograph. It reminded me of the Wop—and the stuff he'd pulled in Tia Juana, with Cards Ganlin fighting him all the way. The renegade Mex had had things pretty much his way, along the Border, until Ben Breed had sat in on the game. And Cards Ganlin, himself a crook, was helping us just so long as the Wop had power—we both knew that. After the Wop went out—

Ben Breed finished speaking. He looked me in the eyes. His own gray eyes held a peculiar, cold expression.

"It's our best chance, Mac," he said slowly. "The Wop's not after money—this time. He's after—*us!*"

I stared down at the sketch of the plane, nodded.

"You're the boss, Ben," I said slowly. "But remember this—at some point in the game, Cards Ganlin'll quit us. He's looking out for himself."

Ben Breed smiled coldly. He shoved the envelope in his pocket. The muscles of his lean, browned face relaxed.

"He won't quit us—yet!" he said slowly. "And when he *does* quit—"

Breed stopped speaking, stiffened. He leaned down, blew out the lamp. We both stood motionless, listening intently. From the outside of the 'dobe shack, softly, sounded a whistle. It was a strange whistle—like that of a bird, a parrot. I'd heard *El Pajaro* whistle that way. And Ben Breed had whistled that way. And now—a third human was doing it.

There was a grip on my arm. Ben's lips were close to my right ear, He spoke in a faint whisper.

"Quiet! Get back—of the table!"

I moved in that direction. I heard Ben draw in his breath. And then, from his lips, came another whistle. It was similar to the one we had just heard, only pitched higher. I crouched back of the table, in the semi-darkness, raised my Colt. There was a faint light near the step—and the body of *El Pajaro*. I heard footfalls—very faint. And then I heard thick tones from the lips of Ben Breed. It might have been *El Pajaro* speaking again, from the dead. The same slurring, half-lisping voice the Mexican had possessed.

"Come, Señor—it is well!"

I waited, scarcely breathing. Somehow, I sensed that it was the Wop who would enter. Antonio Flores. The footfalls had ceased. And suddenly, it crashed—once, twice, three times! Red split the gloom of the larger room. I squeezed the trigger of my forty-five. It filled the smaller room with its roar. I heard a hoarse cry from Ben Breed, heard his body batter down to the soft earth—saw the shape of it as he fell.

And from the other room there was a laugh—a terrible laugh. The Wop's laugh.

"Si, Señor—it is well!" he chuckled—and as my gun crashed again toward the room and a figure I did not see, the laughter died—there was the sound of running feet on the planks.

I straightened, my heart pounding furiously. Three shots—the Wop had fired—straight at Ben Breed. And Ben had crashed down to the earth of the little 'dobe shack's room.

"Damn him!" I muttered. "He played his—"

"Steady!" The voice came from the earth before me. Ben's voice, calm—sharp as a knife. "Don't go—outside!"

I was at his side. "He missed?" I muttered. "He didn't—"

I stopped asking questions. Ben Breed was up on his knees, staring at the door in the next room. He spoke in a whisper.

"I was down—under the first shot. He knew—*El Pajaro* was dead, Mac. He knew!"

I swore softly. Breed imitating the voice of a man the Wop knew could never speak again!

"How?" I whispered.

Ben Breed got to his feet. "We'll know *that*—before we get out of Juarez!" he muttered grimly. "We'll *have* to know it—to *get* out."

I stared toward the opening in the baked clay. Sounds from the main avenue drifted into the tiny room.

"You mean—" I asked slowly—"we're trapped?"

Ben Breed's reply was direct enough, His voice was very low.

"He hasn't seen me—dead!" he stated. "You turned loose lead at him. He'll stick—and he won't be alone!"

I groaned. "We waited—too long!" I muttered.

Breed was silent for a few seconds. When he spoke his voice was very low.

"No choice. If we'd gone out—it would have been the finish. They won't rush in—and we won't rush out."

I swore softly. "Ben—" I muttered—"They've got us—"

Breed gripped my left wrist. It hurt—that grip.

"Cut it!" he snapped. "Somewhere inside—the Wop's yellow! And somewhere outside—there's Cards Ganlin! We're fighting, see?"

I got control of myself. Breed took his long fingers off my wrist. He swore harshly.

"Not in a dirty shack—I *don't* get mine!" he whispered grimly. "I'll take mine in the sky—in a ship—with wings—"

I thought of the envelope in Breed's pocket, thought of the sketch.

"With—red wings!" I muttered thickly, and stared at Breed.

His gray eyes were half closed. He nodded his head slowly, smiled with tight lips.

"Better than—*this* way!" he breathed fiercely. "With red wings!"

IT WAS GETTING dark outside. Twice Mexicans had come into the shack, calling for *El Pajaro*. In neither instance had the men moved toward the back room. The bar in the larger room was small; *El Pajaro* had had no help. He made only a bare living with the cerveza and hot liquors; we both knew that.

We waited. Guns in our laps—we sat in the cool damp of the room—and waited. And after a long silence Ben Breed spoke. His voice was quiet, husky.

"After dark—we get clear," he said slowly. "Cards Ganlin may have lost you—when his man got knifed. We can't stay here too long."

I didn't reply. The Wop knew so many things. Ben figured that he had known *El Pajaro* was dead. And yet he had whistled—like a bird. He had almost trapped Breed. And Ben's imitation of the dead Mexican's voice had been perfect. Yes, the Wop must have known.

Ten minutes passed. Through the space between the adobe walls we could see figures pass—not many of them. Mexicans using the mean street. It was almost dark now.

Breed straightened suddenly. A shape was before the door of the shack. A man entered. He came in very slowly, turned his head toward the bar. He was tall and thin, and he kept his left hand in a pocket of his coat. He wore no hat.

A laugh sounded, somewhere out in the street. Ben Breed swore sharply. The man in the other room whirled. He went down on his knees—the hand came out of his pocket. A gun crashed. The man got to his feet. He had a gun of his own— and it crackled twice. He staggered toward the door. He was just outside when he dropped again.

His body curled in the dirt of the narrow street. From the distance came the sudden clatter of shots—higher pitched. I was on my feet.

"Steady!" Breed's voice was grim. "That's a shooting gallery— with a customer. One of the Wop's men—"

I tried to steady my nerves. "The last time—I didn't hear it—"

Ben spoke slowly. "That try for me—it wasn't in the books," he stated. "They were waiting—for this one!"

I stared out into the street. Once again my nerves were on edge. It was the waiting—the sticking in the 'dobe shack.

"The *policia*—there might be some on the main stem—" Ben's voice was low—"and the shooting at clay—that helps."

"Cards Ganlin!" I muttered. "It looked like—"

"It wasn't!" Ben snapped. "Cards wouldn't play that way. He'd look—"

He stopped speaking. The shooting gallery was in action again. From the distance we could hear the clang of the bell—when a bull's-eye was made. It sounded as though more than one customer were shooting. Ben Breed spoke sharply.

"That's funny—if the Wop—"

It beat down Ben's words—the staccato roar from the street. In a flash we were both lying flat on our stomachs—in the soft earth. And a stream of machine-gun bullets was tearing through the narrow entrance to the shack. Baked clay spurted; splinters spouted up from the plank floor. A bullet tore into the earth less than two feet from my face. I rolled over toward Ben. He was swearing fiercely.

And then, as suddenly as it had started, the clatter of the machine-gun fire died. Voices sounded from the distance—in Mex. I wiped some dirt from my lips. Ben Breed was raising his head.

"That's the finish, Mac!" he muttered. "That racket'll attract too much attention for the Wop to—"

A few shots sounded—not the high-pitched shooting gallery cracks. They were nearer than that. Somewhere out in the street. Voices were coming closer. Breed stood up.

"The officials'll be in here—in a hurry!" he muttered. "We've got to duck, Mac. I'll go first—you follow me. I'll head for the main stem. Safer. Keep your Colt under cloth—and use your eyes!"

The street was deserted as we moved along. Breed was fifty yards ahead of me—and we kept close to the baked clay of shacks all the way, until Breed made another turn—and we were on a lighted street.

He slowed down, and I reached his side. His face seemed grayer, his eyes older—more tired. But he smiled faintly.

"Nearly got you bumped out that time, Mac," he stated. "The Wop's desperate. If you want to wing out of this thing—"

I swore. "I'm still behind, Ben," I muttered. "I owe him something. What do we do—"

Ben gripped my arm; his eyes were staring across the lighted street, toward a bar. The place was doing a big business; it was near the main street—and the Border closed at nine. El Paso folks were thirsty. But it wasn't the crowd moving both ways through the small, swinging doors that Breed was staring at. It was on a figure moving across the street toward us that his gray eyes widened, then narrowed. I drew a deep breath. The man was Cards Ganlin!

He came toward us, his gambler's face expressionless. Both hands were in sight—fingers opened. He halted before Ben.

"Thought the Wop got you!" he muttered. He had come out from the bar, but he was breathing heavily. "He got Rickers—and the Bird. He's raising hell—I cut my hand, sketched the ship—"

"Know that." Breed cut in sharply. "I got your envelope—with the ship. Someone knifed the Mex who was trailing Mac—"

"I know *that!*" Ganlin interrupted hoarsely. "Get this, Breed—the Wop's got your ship wing-painted red. There's a Federal army plane due in Juarez tonight. A Mex army officer by the name of Aguerro is flying her—a captain. It's a recruiting stunt. Her wings are red—"

Ben Breed stiffened. The crowd was surging past the three of us. I got my back to the wall, and kept my eyes opened. Ganlin was using his eyes, too.

"Why—" Ben muttered—"is the Wop flying the new paint—"

"Aguerro trailed the Wop and his outfit through Jalisco for two months, not so long ago," Ganlin cut in, speaking rapidly. "Flores was playing the bandit out in the open. Aguerro killed off half of his band—he damn near got the Wop. Flores knows that the captain's coming in. I'm not on to the game—but something's due for a break."

Breed nodded. "You're good to us, Cards," he stated in a hard voice. "Playing us against—"

"Hell!" Ganlin's tone was grim as he cut in on Breed. "The Wop's got the town loaded. I need every break—"

Breed laughed harshly. His gray eyes bored into the eyes of the gambler.

"Where's the ship?" he snapped. "My ship?"

Cards Ganlin lowered his head. He spoke with his eyes on the broken pavement.

"Half mile west of town—just back of the Rio's mud flats—this side. She's covered with mesquite stuff—came in last night. I'm telling you—something's on—"

Breed nodded. "If he's playing for this Aguerro—"

Ganlin swore hoarsely. "More than that," he stated. "I nearly got him—while he had machine-guns up to wipe you out in *El Pajaro's* place. He's stronger than the Mex police—right now. I've given it to you straight—I'm sliding out—"

He half turned. Ben Breed chuckled hoarsely. He spoke in a steady voice.

"*Maybe* you are, Cards—don't count on me. I'm doing the same thing."

Ganlin smiled. It was a tight-lipped smile, without mirth. He spoke so that I could just catch his words.

"Half mile—back of the flats. On the straight, Breed—red wings—"

And then he was merged into the mixed crowd of Americanos and greasers, and Ben Breed was lighting a black-papered pill. I stared at it.

"Where in hell—" I muttered—"did you get *those?*"

Ben grinned. "From the table," he said grimly. "Back in the shack. When the Wop's around I don't leave anything—behind!"

THERE WAS A lot of excitement along the main stem. We stopped at the Green Fan, and Ben talked to an American bartender. I stood back of the swinging doors—and watched the crowd. There was a lot of bum music drifting around, and plenty of smells. I didn't particularly object to either—it was good to be able to listen, and breathe through my nose. Ben came up behind me.

"Big shooting over on a back street," he stated, as if he were giving me some news. "They've found two dead men—and they picked up a Mex who'd been knifed, just before the shooting. The *Jefe de Policia* is worried as hell—because one Captain

Ramon Aguerro is flying into town, and there's a celebration on for him. The *Jefe* figures there's some *revolutionaires* hanging around."

I didn't say a thing. Ben lowered his voice.

"We're going back across the Rio, Mac," he said. "We're doing some air business—and in a hurry."

I stared at Ben. His eyes held a peculiar expression.

"We're going to take a crack at your ship?" I asked. "Not so good. If we wait until this Aguerro comes in—the Wop'll go after him, and we'll be sitting where—"

"I'm making a guess, Mac"—Ben was smiling—"that Captain Aguerro won't wing in to Jaurez tonight. He'd have been in by this time—unless he had engine trouble. And when he set that ship down, one of two things happened. He decided to keep her down until he got light—or the *Jefe de Policia* got word to him."

My eyes narrowed. A taxi rattled along near the curb. Breed signaled the driver. The door opened—he shoved me in, got in after me. The driver was Mex, and he had nice white teeth.

"The El Paso!" Ben told him. "Make it fast!"

The cab couldn't do that but the driver did the best he could. Traffic was heavy; the street was narrow, and there were the street cars blocking us. We had three squares to go, and then a turn to the right—and northward across the Rio. We made the three squares. I was watching the crowd when the cab turned—to the left! Not toward the river, but *away* from it!

I stiffened. Ben Breed moved his right arm. He jerked up his automatic. The window that separated us from the driver was half opened. Ben's voice sounded, sharply.

"Stop! Turn her—or I'll—"

The brakes squealed. The driver turned his head—saw the gun. He slipped down in the seat. Ben leaned forward.

A figure swung out from the curb. The man was short, and had a dark hat pulled down over his forehead. He raised his right arm—I pulled Ben down in the seat. There was the pop-cough of a Maxim-silenced gun—once, twice. Material in the cab shivered. The driver muttered in his native language. I twisted, jerked my Colt free—

The short one with the black hat was gone. Ben shoved open the door, slid to the street. Mexicans were crowding about the cab—there was a lot of jabbering. I followed Ben out—he led the way across the street. We got into the crowd. A street car came along, slowly. Ben swung aboard. I followed him. We moved up front in the car. For the first time, Ben spoke.

"He's still in Jaurez, Mac—and he knows we're going out, now. We've got to move fast."

I nodded. Breed shook his head slowly.

"Might have known that cab driver was in the deal," he muttered. "Got him too easily—he was anxious—"

"Ben—" I interrupted grimly—"the Wop's damned anxious to have us out of the way. Something *is* on—Cards Ganlin was right."

The lean face of Breed held a tense expression. He nodded his head slowly.

"He can't afford to be wrong—not much!" Ben spoke grimly. "I was sure the Wop would play Juarez, after the Bisbee deal. But I didn't know anything about this Aguerro angle. Cards would know—he was close to Flores once."

The street car rattled across the west bridge in the loop system. The river was dark-gray, below. Ben spoke in a steady tone.

"We'll make the field, Mac—and ride the two-seater up. That ship's worth coin to me—the single-seater. But the Wop's worth more. It was self-defense, over there. We've got to get him—before he gets us. We'll take up some of Jake's flares. If we can get down and take off the single-seater—we'll do it. If not—you do your stuff. Riddle her with the Lewis-gun. More chance of getting the Wop—with the ship out of commission."

I nodded. And then I thought about Cards Ganlin.

"Cards—" I said slowly—"he's playing in this game. He might have something to gain—if there *weren't* any red-winged ship over there back of the mud flats."

Ben Breed swore. His eyes were narrowed to little gray slits.

"Mac," he said slowly, "when you're sitting in a game with two crooks—both of 'em clever—you never can tell. But if you get a hand—you play it. Ganlin's a double-crosser—so's the Wop. Flores held the cards—across the river. He came damn close to taking all the chips. He didn't. Maybe Cards let us see his hand—*maybe* he didn't. My guess is that we hold something—and we play 'em that way."

The street car slowed down for the inspection on the American side. I drew a deep breath.

"We've *got* to hold something," I muttered harshly, "*this* time! I'm hoping it's a pair of—red wings!"

Ben was smiling coldly.

THE MEX NEWSBOYS were yelling their heads off over in El Paso. We climbed into a cab, had the driver zig-zag through traffic for a few minutes—and then headed for the field. Joe Picket was watching the ship. He grinned at us.

"How's things going across the stream?" he asked. "No celebration, eh? Not with this guy Aguerro down in a crash."

We stared at him. He had a paper with a short bulletin to the effect that Captain Ramon Aguerro had crashed near a mountain town, about forty miles from Juarez—southward. It was reported that the Federal captain was badly hurt.

I climbed into the rear cockpit while Joe was jerking the blocks from the front wheels. Ben Breed got into the front cockpit, adjusted his helmet and goggles, and snapped the ignition switch. He didn't rev the engine up in a roar—but it was warming up with a low rumble as I got the canvas off the Lewis-gun and inspected it. She looked right—and I slipped on a drum. Then I pulled my helmet and goggles on. Five minutes passed. Joe stood up on a wing-step and talked to Ben. I guessed that he was asking questions—and not learning much.

Ben jerked his head. "We'll get right to our spot Mac," he called above the rumble of the engine. "After that—we'll see what happens."

I nodded, made sure that the rip-cord of my Irving 'chute was set for action, over my left thigh. The two-seater rolled out into the wind. Her rumble became a roar—we climbed off the field, got altitude. About two thousand feet of it. Then Ben winged her west of El Paso, crossing the lighted town. He banked—we roared over the Rio. Then he cut the throttle—and we started to glide.

We both saw it—at the same instant. A red trail in the sky—just off the earth below. The exhaust stream of a plane!

Ben twisted in the front cockpit. He shouted above the shrill of the wires.

"Watch him, Mac! I'm diving—to make sure—"

I nodded my head, swung the bracketed Lewis-gun. The Wop had Ben's stolen single-seater—a faster ship, with a Browning prop-synchronized. But we had altitude, and Ben could handle even as ancient a crate as the two-seater we had picked up. We came down with wires screaming. I stared over the side. And suddenly there was a white light—drifting. A flare—Ben had let loose a flare! Below it, climbing in a spiral, was a swift, red-winged single-seater!

I swore hoarsely. The single-seater was zooming up at us. Red trailed out from her nose. Above the roar of the two-seater's engine sounded the more staccato clatter of Browning fire. Ben banked our ship—I let the Lewis-gun pump lead downward, over the slanted fuselage. The Wop had been short—he let his plane fall off on a wing as the Lewis-gun bullets streamed down at him.

And then, suddenly, Ben was twisting in the front cockpit—pointing, with an arm out in the prop wash, above us. I stared upward—the sky burst into a flare of white. Shapes were plunging down. One of them came into the glare of light. A red-winged single-seater! Not the Wop's plane—she was below. Another plane!

Ben zoomed the two-seater. He waved his left arm furiously. The single-seater above was diving straight at us—red streaked down as she curved upward, holding her altitude. Another flare burst into white light. Another ship streaked down from an angle. *She* had red wings, too—and was a single-seater!

Ben let the two-seater fall off on a wing. Her nose came down. A shape flashed up from below—struts splintered out near the left wing-tip as the Wop squeezed the stick-trigger of the Browning. I shouted hoarsely.

"Wing out! He tricked—"

Ben was letting the battered two-seater spin now. She was down to a thousand feet. I stared at the left wing, wondering if it would start to warp. The two-seater came out of the spin— Ben slanted her toward the lights of El Paso. The river was below—a faintly-gleaming, winding stream of water.

Ben's head was turned toward the rear cockpit. He screamed at me as the two-seater dived.

"Aguerro—thinks we're—the Wop!"

Then his head was to the front again. A red-winged single-seater was diving down at us. I waved my arms—but it might be the Wop. I couldn't take the chance of waiting. The bracketed Lewis-gun swung out. The red-winged ship zoomed—her tracer stream was short. As she went up a shape flashed down through the white light of two flares. I swore harshly. The fuselage was round, different from the other shapes. And a red stream traced downward—battered into the fuselage of the zooming Federal plane. There was a burst of flame. One red-winged ship twisted toward the Rio. The other roared upward, leveled off—then headed westward along the line—with two other planes in pursuit.

Ben Breed was winging the two-seater northward now. He was across the river—heading back of El Paso. The city was to the east of our course. I looked at the shattered strut. We were down within a few hundred feet of the earth. Ben turned his head. He cut down the engine speed.

"We'll land—away from El Paso—there'll be hell to pay—"

I nodded, twisted my head to the westward. I could see the exhaust streams of three ships. And I could see that the one furthest west was gaining rapidly on the other two. I spoke thickly to myself, through oil-stained lips.

"Once again—the Wop's getting clear!"

THE TWO-SEATER RESTED on a level stretch. Scattered mesquite dotted the spot where we had come down. There were no ranch lights in sight— we were perhaps fifty miles northwest of El Paso and Juarez. Ben and I sat with our backs propped up against the tail assembly of the two-seater. It was Ben who spoke.

"Aguerro never did crash in Mexico, Mac," he stated grimly. "He had word that the Wop was in town. He was coming in to get him. The Federal Government want him—and want him badly. Aguerro was trying to trick him. But he didn't know that the Wop had red wings. And Flores must have figured that Aguerro would try the very stunt he did. He was flying a ship painted like the Federal planes—and they were after *us*—after our *white* wings. That is—they were until the Wop shot down one of their pilots. It might have been Aguerro—more likely it wasn't. Flores' a tough one, Mac. He's a fighting Wop!"

I smiled grimly. "He *might* have figured that we'd come after him," I muttered. "Cards gave us that tip—it wasn't so good. Supposing he's sitting in with—"

I stopped. Ben Breed closed his gray eyes, laughed harshly. He spoke in his husky tone.

"They're *both* crooks, Mac," he stated. "There'll be a fuss over this thing. We'll stay in the clear. The Wop'll stay in the clear—for a week or so. Those ships can't catch that plane of mine. He didn't get coin on this deal. He was trying for a kill. He's *got* to have coin."

I nodded. My lips moved slowly. I was pretty tired, let down.

"Can we *stop* him from getting it, Ben?" I asked in a low tone.

Ben Breed opened his gray eyes. They glinted in the first light of a rising moon. He spoke in a steady voice.

"If we *don't*, Mac," he stated grimly, "just one other thing will happen. He'll stop *us* from stopping *him!*"

Ghost Guns

A Federal agent and an ex-flyer team together to get a much wanted bandit; and, as sometimes happens, the pursued turns pursuer.

TICARDI ISN'T MUCH of a town. A main street lined with wooden and 'dobe shacks, dirty and hot; brown-gray hills sprawling to the south and southwest; a winding railroad track separating it from the U.S.A., over which one train a day runs; sand and mesquite—gambling houses. And stakes for the pikers.

Ticardi can't compete with Tia Juana, less than eighty miles westward, and thus it doesn't get the tourist crowd. Nor a certain type of crook. But it's a bad town. Cheap and ugly; bad in a snarling sort of way, if you get what I mean.

I sat in the lobby of the Red House, back from the narrow door that was the main entrance, and looked out along the street. It was my idea that Ben Breed had pulled a bad one; Ticardi didn't seem to be the sort of town the Wop could use in his business. My hunch was that Flores had winged back toward Tia Juana, and that we were wasting time sticking in a small-time drinking and gambling spot. But Ben Breed was the boss, and things had been so tough up at El Paso and Juarez, two days ago, that I was willing to let him *stay* boss.

The Wop was scrapping us now. Us—and Cards Ganlin. Up until two days ago he'd gone about his business of sticking up banks for coin, playing both sides of the Line, and weeding out the squealers in his ranks at the same time. But we'd queered his game a few times, and so had Cards Ganlin. So now the Wop was trying to get us—and coming pretty close to succeeding. So close that we'd cut out looking like our natural selves. It was uncomfortable, but safer.

Ben Breed was down looking up a Mex by the name of Morello. He'd gone alone—pasty-faced, the muscles of his mouth twitching constantly, his hands never still. He had all the signs of one who used snow, and he was ragged in attire. I was playing it the other way—a Mex dude, all spruced up to hell. Stain on my face, neck, arms and hands—a snappy duck suit, brown shoes. Flaming socks and a tie with two colors, either one of which could dazzle. I was selling a new-fangled roulette wheel, but my samples hadn't come in yet. They never would come in.

I sat on the hard chair and pulled on an *Elegante*. Across the street from the Red House, which was the only two-story shack in town, was *La Fonda Bar*. It was around noon, and the hottest time of the day for drinking. The place was pretty crowded, but most of the customers were Mex. I got to thinking about this Morello. He'd quit the Wop a long time ago, according to Ben. The chances were he didn't know a thing. But Ben never bothered about the chances. The Wop had a habit of never forgetting those who had worked with him. Morello had a beer shack in Ticardi, and wasn't doing so badly.

Ben remembered that—and he figured that if *he* remembered it perhaps the Wop would. Thus he was somewhere in town, looking up Morello. I yawned and hoped he'd learn nothing much. I didn't like Ticardi, and any moment I expected someone to come in making a lot of noise that would prove to me that the Wop was in Tia Juana for a gambling house stick-up or a kill. Flores was well known on this side of the Line, and when the Mexicans get news they make a holiday of it.

A Mex came out of the swinging door in front of *La Fonda*. He was a pretty big man, and he was grinning broadly. He wore a battered *sombrero*, a drooping *mustachio*, a soiled shirt, faded yellow pants—and highly-shined yellow shoes. He stood for a few seconds in the white dust of the street, wiping a big mouth with a sleeve. I looked at him and yawned.

A short Mex was heading for the bar shack. He carried a big bundle in front of him, using both arms. I couldn't see his face. The big Mex raised a hand and shoved back his *sombrero*. His forehead gleamed in the sun. He started to stretch.

There was a crash behind me, in the lobby. I twisted my head, and my right hand dropped down a few inches lower. Two voices started chattering at the same time. On the wood floor near the counter that served as a desk, were the remnants of a water pitcher. Pedro had fallen asleep while walking, and it had slipped out of his grip. I couldn't exactly blame the Mex who did about everything around the hotel. I turned my head toward the street again. My nerves were not so good.

What I saw didn't help them any. The big Mex who had

been stretching when I'd jerked my head around—he was still stretching. Only this time he was doing a complete job of it. His body was sprawled out in the yellow dust—and it wasn't moving. The little Mex was entering the bar shack, still gripping his bundle in both arms. He vanished from sight behind the doors that swung closed after him. I got up from the hard chair, headed for the door.

Then I changed my mind. There were several Mexicans, and one American, heading toward the motionless figure. The American wasn't Ben Breed. He was fat, and sloppy looking. His face was as white as the heat in the town. Perspiration dripped down it; I could see that from the hotel doorway.

The proprietor of the hotel was still chattering excitedly about the broken water pitcher. I went past the two Mexicans, got out the back way, into an alley. Then I circled around and reached the main street. There were six or seven humans gathered around the figure in the dust. More were arriving with every second that passed. I put on a slight swagger and reached the group. The fat American was talking. He was talking shakily.

"I seen him—standin' here—stretchin'. Then someone knocks a beer glass off the bar back of me. I was over to the O'Brien shack. I turns—an' when I looks back—he's lyin' like this."

I stared down. There were two holes in the big man's forehead. One was about an inch from the other. They showed redly in the hot sunlight, as he lay on his back. The fat American spoke again.

"He's dead, all right. An' if that beer glass hadn't busted I'd have been lookin' right at—"

I turned away. There was something funny about the way the

thing had happened. Funny in a grim way, that is. Two of us looking right at the big Mexican, as he stood there stretching. A beer glass topples off a bar—and the fat one looks away. A water pitcher crashes on the floor of the Red House, and *I* look away.

But I'd seen the short Mex moving toward *La Fonda*. He'd had a large bundle in his arms. The fat American must have seen him, too. I lighted a new pill, and waited for him to say something about that. He didn't. And that struck me as being sort of strange.

The one with the bundle had fired the two shots that had crashed the big Mexican down. I was sure of that. The shooting had been too accurate—no one else was close enough. There had been no reports from the gun. Maxim-silenced, that would mean. And the big Mex certainly hadn't been expecting the lead. He'd acted as though he hadn't a worry in the world. He hadn't—now.

I stared down the street. A figure was walking up toward the group, walking shakily. The man's face was white, pasty. His hands shook as they clutched at his tattered, light coat. It was Ben Breed. He halted near me, staring down toward the road. He didn't speak.

Someone cursed, and I swung around. From the swinging door of *La Fonda* came a short Mex. In his arms he held a large bundle. I stiffened. The crowd gathered about the body gave way. The short Mex dropped the bundle. He cried out hoarsely. Then he ran forward, dropped on his knees. He talked excitedly, and his voice was filled with passion.

The big American moved toward me. He was shaking his head. I came pretty close to speaking to him, in English. Then

I remembered the brown stain on my face and hands. I wasn't supposed to do much talking. And the roulette wheel sales line that Ben had taught me didn't fit in here.

I couldn't get the thing straight. The man kneeling beside the dead Mex looked a lot like the one I'd seen moving toward him, before the pitcher had dropped. He carried the same bundle, unless the heat was getting me. If *he* hadn't fired the two shots—

"What's wrong, Mister?" Ben Breed whined the words at the fat American. That individual was rolling a yellow-papered cigarette. He talked more to himself than to Ben.

"Funny as hell! Sure is—some gent rubbed Morello out!"

I saw Ben jerk a bit. And the name stiffened me up. Morello—the one he was looking for in Ticardi!

The big American moved back across the street, shaking his head. Ben Breed moved closer to the motionless form in the street. A khaki-clad Mex member of the *polizio* was running up, breathing hard. Ben Breed moved back of me. He muttered just one word.

"Room!"

Then he walked unsteadily down the street, away from the Red House. I stood in the same spot I'd been standing—and listened to the excited jabberings of the short Mex. His bundle was laying over near the swing doors of the bar. It would take Ben a few minutes to circle around and get back to the hotel. I moved toward the bundle.

A dirty-faced Mex caught me by the arm and said something about something I didn't understand. I got loose, moved toward *La Fonda* again—and pulled up short. The bundle had vanished!

The doors were swinging—but no legs showed beneath them. I decided not to go inside. There were a few things that bothered me. The one Breed had been searching for had been crashed down. And the one I figured had done the crashing down was acting up pretty badly right now. A fat American had used the term "rubbed out" pretty casual-like, and hadn't said anything about seeing the one with the bundle. He wasn't blind—this American—and I didn't rate him as being dumb.

I decided to get back to our room in the Red House. And I decided some other things. Ben Breed hadn't been so dumb in heading for Ticardi. Where there was smoke—

My ears hadn't picked up even the spit-cough of a Maxim-silenced gun. The falling pitcher wouldn't have drowned the sound of *two* shots. And it might have been an accident. The beer glass thing might have happened—or it might have been an out for the fat American. I guessed that it had happened— he'd play safe in case of a check-up. Though the chances of there being much of a check-up in a spot like Ticardi weren't great.

I reached the coop that Ben and I were using, though the proprietor thought otherwise. He figured I was the sole occupant—Antonio Gomez, dealer in trick roulette wheels. The door was slightly opened—I kicked it the rest of the way open, walked in. Ben kicked it closed—from behind. He spoke in a low tone.

"Who got him, Mac?"

I shook my head. The blinds of the one window were drawn. Voices drifted up from the hot street.

"She didn't bark, Ben," I muttered. "Two bullets—and I didn't hear either of 'em depart."

Ben Breed nodded his head slowly. He spoke in a husky voice, his gray eyes narrowed.

"Ghost guns in town, eh? What's your *guess?*"

"The little Mex who came out and got excited—he passed the big boy, just before that gent did the crash—"

Ben swore softly. "Sure?" he muttered.

I shook my head. "Not positive," I stated. "Same build—only saw his back, before the shoot. Had a bundle—"

"Juan Morello!" Ben cut in sharply. "That short bird's his brother, Mac—"

I stared at Ben Breed. I thought of the bundle, the build of the one who had carried it across the street, through the swinging doors. My eyes hadn't been turned away for more than six or seven seconds. Maybe ten.

"This Juan—he's all right?" I asked grimly. "Wouldn't knock off his own—"

Ben Breed frowned. "Crazy over his brother, Mac—he was hunting him up for me. Talked with him, thirty minutes ago. Went down toward the old mine, myself, looking for him. Juan was going to hunt him up in town—"

I shook my head slowly. "They switched the bundle, Ben," I muttered. "But why?"

He ignored my second question, and asked me one in a low, grim tone.

"*Who* switched the bundle, Mac?"

I smiled grimly. "One of the boys in on the Maxim-silencer kill," I said slowly.

Ben Breed frowned. He was silent for several minutes. Then he narrowed his gray eyes on mine.

"Mac—" he said slowly—"we're taking a licking. The Wop's

out to get us. He's somewhere around Ticardi, and he isn't after coin. He's after us—and maybe Cards Ganlin. I played as though I were filled with green beer, going into Morello's shack. But I kept my eyes opened. Two gents—both Mex—slid out right away. I warned Juan to go at it easy-like. Now his brother's out of things. Mac—how'd you like to let me fly you up to San Diego?"

I stared at Ben. "Why?" I asked.

"Just to loaf around," Ben came back. "Your share of the reward coin on the recovery of that first Wop stick-up money—it'll be enough for a plane buy. And you can joy-hop around—"

I got sore. "I'm sticking, Ben," I muttered. "Told you that, up at Juarez, when things were a whole lot worse than they are—"

Ben cut in. "They're pretty bad—right now! We're spotted. The ship's down four miles across the Line. Morello's rubbed out—"

"If we're spotted—why didn't they get us when we were both together out there?" I interrupted.

Ben grunted. "The Federal police want The Wop—and want him badly," he reminded. "He can't come right out in the open. Got to be a bit delicate, Mac."

I grinned. The Wop's delicacy was almost funny.

"All right," I conceded. "They got your man, Morello. That fat American looks a bit pale around the gills. Notice that?"

Ben Breed frowned. He swore softly.

"He *did* look that way," he agreed. "Right now it's ten to one he looks *red* around the gills!"

I stiffened. Ben was shaking his head slowly.

"He talked too much—right out in the street. He knew Morello had been rubbed out—and his fear of something else let him act careless. He's done."

I swore softly. "Know him?" I asked.

Ben nodded. "I *knew* him," he stated. "Used to be bank teller up at Douglas. Name's Porgnan—Louis. Got gambling across the Line—ducked out with twenty grand. They never did get him."

I stiffened. "*You* can get him—now!" I breathed.

Ben Breed grunted again. His voice was husky, low.

"He's finished by this time, Mac—you don't seem, to get that—"

He stopped talking. We both reached down toward our guns. There had sounded a knock on the door. Outside we could hear heavy breathing. Ben moved toward one wall—I backed up toward the other. The muzzle of my Colt rubbed the cloth of the inner side of a coat pocket. Neither of us spoke. A fist pounded on the door. A voice called out.

"Señor Gomez!"

I looked across the narrow room at Ben. He nodded his head, pointing toward the bed. I walked over and eased down on it. Then I sat up, called out sleepily.

"Hello! Someone—call?"

I yawned nervously. Ben was sliding along the wall toward the door. The voice outside sounded again.

"It's Davis—Johnny Davis. I would do business with you in my gambling place. One of your wheels—"

Ben nodded to me. The door wasn't locked. We both had pretty sharp ears.

"Come on in!" I called.

The door opened. I sat up on the bed, mussing up my hair a bit. It took all I had to keep my gun fingers outside of my duck coat pocket. But Ben was set for a shoot—that helped. The door opened all the way—and Ben was back of it. A big form blocked the entrance. Porgnan—the fat American!

He moved forward slowly. There was a smile on his face. The sun slanted in through the blinds. I yawned again. Porgnan spoke.

"It's no good," he stated in a peculiar tone. "You saw that kill—an' you don't sleep that easily."

I tried to look as though I didn't think he were right, but it wasn't much of a success. He'd seen me down in the street, less than ten minutes ago. I did some quick thinking. Even if he weren't wise to the fact that I wasn't a Mex selling roulette wheels, he must be pretty suspicious. I'd told him to "come on in"—and that hadn't been so good. But he'd talked English to me, which showed he figured I could understand.

He acted pretty nervous, and he left the door of the room opened. I kept my eyes on the narrow hallway beyond the room. There was a skylight above the hallway, and yellow light dropped down on the rough boards of the floor. I commenced to feel like a trapped rat.

"I don't lose much sleep over a shooting, Mr. Davis," I stated. "You wanted to talk with me?"

He looked around the room, and didn't see Ben Breed. Ben's length and leanness allowed him to flatten out pretty well, back of the door.

The big American made a swift movement with his right hand. I didn't even have a chance to get my fingers in the right side pocket of my duck coat. Porgnan had a nasty-looking gun pointed in my direction, but it wasn't a ghost gun. No Maxim silencer on it.

"You may lose some sleep over *this* one, Breed!" he snapped. "But there's an out."

I felt my heart pounding, and my throat was too tight for easy words. The big gent was mistaking me for Ben Breed!

There was a little silence. Down in the street, voices were raised, talking in Mex. A tinny piano rattled in the usual way, inside one of the beer shacks.

I looked at the big American and his mean-looking gun, and saw the door back and slightly to one side of him move the fraction of an inch.

"An out?" I muttered pretty thickly. "What is it, Porgnan?"

He stiffened at the name, and his gun hand jerked a little. In the slanting light from the blinds, his face was a white mask, cut into slices of light and dark.

"I'm *Davis!*" he muttered. "The Wop's out for a kill. I'm telling you his hang-out. You get him before he gets me—that's the out!"

I swore softly. The big American was as yellow as the sun spot on the rough boards of the floor. I nodded my head slowly.

"But—get this!" The man who insisted he was Davis had a snarl in his voice. He was growing excited. "You rub him out—all the way, see! No steel-cuff take—no riding across the Line with him. You use lead!"

I nodded. "Act natural, Porgnan!" I snapped, taking my play from him. "There's only one way to get Flores—you know that."

His pasty face held a slight smile. It was twisted, grim. He nodded, lowered his gun just a little.

"All right, Breed!" he muttered. "I've kept clear of you for a long time—and you'll have your hands full with the Wop—now. I'll be gone after the kill. But I'll be back of you—*until* the shoot, get that!"

I nodded. "I want the Wop, Porgnan—not you!" I snapped. "Where do I—"

The big American swore grimly. "Back of *La Fonda* there's a 'dobe shack. I got a Mex spottin' it. The Wop's inside. You can stick in the alley—an' wait for him to come out. *I'll* stick back of you—an' see what happens."

I nodded. "Why in hell don't *you* do the trick, Porgnan?" I asked.

"Easy!" he came back. "I'm thinkin' about after. That's *your* lookout—when the gang starts to run you down."

I nodded again. A trap? Or was Flores really in the 'dobe shack back of *La Fonda?* I thought of the short Mex with the bundle.

"Who got Morello, Porgnan?" I asked slowly. "I was looking for him."

He grinned. "One of the Wop's gunmen," he stated. "He knew you were lookin' for Morello—the Wop did."

"The Mex with the big bundle?" I muttered questioningly.

The big American nodded. "I saw the kill," he stated. "He dropped the bundle—an' had his rods held underneath it. Two silent bullets—an' Morello was down. I went out for a look—and spotted you, Breed. Knew you were on the Wop—an' I can spot stain when I see it."

He was holding his gun lower, but he was still holding it. I swore softly, and Porgnan chuckled a little. He acted pleased with himself.

"That little Mex looked a lot like the one who came back out of *La Fonda*—flopped down beside Morello," I stated slowly. "And he had the same kind of a bundle—"

"The *same* bundle!" Porgnan corrected. "The killer slipped it to Juan—an' when he came out of *La Fonda* he had it in his arms. Framed, see—a couple of Mexicans saw the kill. They'll swear Juan got his own brother."

I sat motionlessly. "You seem to know a lot, Porgnan," I said finally. "How come?"

The big man nodded his head. He had little eyes for such a big head—they glinted.

"I *ran* the show," he said in a flat tone. "It's no good, Breed—running shows for the Wop. Flores knew you were trailing him. He wanted the Mex out of the way—said you knew him, and might hit for Ticardi. I owed Morello a lot of coin—gambling at his place. So the Wop picked me. It isn't the first time he's picked me for jobs—since I—"

He stopped. I nodded. The Wop never forgot, I knew that. He always made use of men who were outside the law.

"Play along, Breed!" There was a touch of sharpness in Porgnan's tone, "I'll play square with you. You've got a plane somewhere around—and a pal watching it. You work that way. I've got a way out of here, myself."

I nodded. Porgnan had run the show for the Wop, but he was double-crossing, taking the safest way out. He'd picked me for Breed, because of a bum stain job. And he knew we had a ship nearby. He wasn't dumb. I'd sized him up right, down below, on the street.

"Come on!" he muttered, and shifted his weapon a little. "I'm getting tired of holding this gat on you—an' Flores may not stick in the 'dobe shack forever."

I got up off the bed. It wasn't any cinch to figure my play—from this point on. But there was Ben Breed, back of the door that Porgnan had left open. It was up to him.

"Lift 'em, Porgy!"

Ben's words were sharp. The big American's form stiffened. I dropped to my knees. Porgnan whirled, raising his gun. Ben squeezed lead. The gun spat and coughed. Porgnan's gun cracked—filled the room with sound. Plaster rattled down from the wall. The ex-teller slumped to the floor.

Breed was up from his knees, beside the door. Two steps, and he had a finger pressed against Porgnan's wrist. He straightened. A shout sounded from below.

"Dead! It's a duck—for us! Had to get him, Mac—or he'd have got me—"

We were outside. Steps sounded on the ancient stairs to the right. Ben grabbed me—and we turned to the left. He slammed the door of the room, back of us. The Red House boasted two stairways; we were using the one we guessed the others *weren't* using. It was an outside flight—and led down to an alley.

At the foot of it, we turned back toward the main street. Ben was smiling grimly.

"Didn't figure he'd shoot, Mac—thought he'd save the lead for you."

I swore softly. "Do we head for the 'dobe shack, back of *La Fonda?*" I muttered.

Above us we could hear curses, exclamations. Ben Breed shook his head.

"We do *not!*" he snapped. "We head across the Line—for the plane!"

I blinked at Ben. "But it's a chance—"

We were moving toward the main street now, and toward the railroad track, too.

"A hell of a chance!" Ben muttered grimly. "Porgy never had guts enough to double up on the Wop. He gave it to you straight about the Morello kill. But he was still sitting in with Flores—you can gamble on that. It was a trap—"

We moved swiftly, keeping our eyes open. And we both had fingers on our weapons. I was soaked in perspiration.

"But he slipped up," I muttered. "He thought you—"

"Porgnan slipped up, all right!" Ben muttered huskily. "But he never thought that you were Ben Breed!"

I stared at Ben. There was a twisted smile on his face. We were nearing the railroad tracks now, mixing in the crowd on the main street.

"He slipped up by watching me head in this direction, and not figuring that I'd double back," Ben stated in a low tone. "When he got in that room he thought you were alone. He took a look around, and was sure of it. He bluffed you—thinking you'd believe he'd play straight—if he were dealing with Breed."

We reached the inspection shacks. Ben spoke cheerfully to the Mexican *officio*.

"Shooting—back in town. Best to clear out, eh?"

The Mex looked us over with squinted eyes. Ben Breed was speaking in a whining voice, his body slumped forward a bit, his hands shaking again. I smiled and nodded my head. The *officio*, grunting, gestured toward Ben, and said something to me in Mex. I played safe, nodding my head and chuckling. We moved on.

The American inspector regarded Ben narrowly. He looked at me with suspicion. We'd come in when a different inspector was on the Line. Ben spoke in a steady voice.

"You're new here—tell Charlie that Ben checked out at

whatever time it is now. There's a little hell breaking loose back over there—"

The expression in the inspector's eyes changed. He looked me over, smiling.

"That brown stain sweats off in the heat," he observed. "All right—go ahead!"

We went ahead. We cut off from the dirt road that approached the Border Line from the northward, moved toward the field of mesquite and sand on which the two-seater was down. Ben kept turning and looking back. Also, he watched the sky.

"We're running out—this time, eh?" I muttered.

Ben grunted. "We were licked before we started, Mac," he stated grimly. "The Wop checked us going in. Cards isn't in town—and the Wop won't stay there. His play is a double one—to get Cards—and to finish us off. Before we grab him. They'll get him word of Porgnan's going out—and he'll figure who did it. We've got to get away—so we can get *back*."

I swore harshly. We moved up a slope of sand and scattered cacti. Then down the other side. Ben stared back at the southern sky. It was so hot I could feel the stain running down over my chest and back. The ship was several miles off.

"There's just one way to get—the Wop—" Ben muttered grimly. "We can't go into his country and beat him at his own game. He's clever—and slippery. But there's one thing he likes—a lot."

"Liquor?" I guessed.

Ben shook his head. "Close—but not close *enough*, Mac—" he stated. "Women."

I groaned. "Hate to play a woman into his hands, Ben—" I muttered. "If he ever got wise—"

Ben Breed smiled grimly. "We're going to do it—if we get out of this mess—"

He broke off, caught me by the arm. Off to the south, not far from the town, a ship was taking off. She was climbing up into the sky, on the Mexican side. She was winging westward.

"Too soon!" I breathed. "He couldn't have got from that 'dobe shack—"

Ben had increased the pace over the sand, through the scraggly mesquite and cacti. He swore harshly.

"He was never *in* the shack, Mac!" he shot at me. "He's up to cut us off now. Keep moving—and when I drop down—you do the same. The Wop played Ticardi with kid gloves—he used guns that were silenced—ghost guns. And he was ready to get away as soon as the play was finished. That's what he is up to do now—finish the play—with us."

The drone of the plane reached us now. We moved as fast as we could, keeping low. The Wop was roaring up into the sky. He knew we were out of Ticardi. He knew Louis Porgnan had been rubbed out of things. I twisted my head.

"Wings aren't red!" I muttered. "Not your ship, Ben!"

Ben Breed didn't look back. But he spoke.

"He's had time—to paint 'em white, Mac. If he spots our two-seater—"

I followed close to Ben. The single-seater in the sky was gaining altitude rapidly. I spoke heavily.

"First time—we ever—ran out on a deal—"

"Here's hoping it isn't—the *last* time!" I heard Ben mutter huskily. "A lot of gents—haven't been—*able*—to run out on— the Wop!"

THE SHIP IN the sky was circling, less than three thousand feet off the earth, perhaps a half mile to the south of the slope on which we'd landed the two-seater. We were within a quarter mile of the slope, and for the last quarter mile we'd been down on our hands and knees, crawling.

We were both pretty nearly all in. Heat—and the mesquite scrubble were two sweet obstacles to lick, and if the pilot of the ship above spotted movement on the ground, and dived the Browning-armed plane on us—

I twisted my neck, swore grimly. The little ship was hovering almost directly over us now, winging in a mild bank. There was a machine-gun mounted in the rear cockpit of the two-seater, but if the Wop spotted her before we got to her it wouldn't do *us* any good. And even if we *did* reach the plane—the single-seater was much faster.

We crawled on, Ben Breed leading the way. Above us, stalking from the sky, droned the little ship. Minutes passed—and the plane circled steadily. It was getting on my nerves—the way the ship seemed to stay in one sky spot, and almost directly over us. We were within two hundred yards of the two-seater now, and we had to crawl over the crest of a mesquite-dotted slope to get near her.

"Maybe he's spotted us, Ben!" I muttered. "Maybe he's waiting—"

Ben shook his head, crawled on. We were near the crest of the slope. And then, suddenly, the drone of the ship in the sky ceased. I tilted my head—the little plane was diving!

I groaned. Ben swore softly. The ship was diving down in a slant, directly over the slope on which we had left the two-seater. We could hear the shrill of the wires, in the wind.

Something black seemed to flash over the side of the plane—Ben swayed to his feet. I shouted for him to get down, but he paid no attention to me.

The earth shook. There was a terrific crash. Half way down the slope there was a great spurt of sand, bits of torn mesquite and cacti. Ben Breed dropped to his knees. The ship held her glide, then banked.

"He's—seen her!" I muttered. "Bombing her—"

Ben turned toward me. His face was twisted. He spoke grimly, but steadily.

"I'm going up, Mac! Are you coming—"

I was on my feet. We both started running down the slope. It would take time to get the ship off, and the chances were that the Wop had more than one bomb. We ran on, bent low. The engine of the single-seater was droning again.

I jerked at the stakes we'd pounded into the ground, at the wing-tips, ripped them loose. Then I ran around back, toward the tail-assembly, and jerked that stake loose from the sand. There was a crater where the bomb had struck, perhaps a hundred yards back of the two-seater. Ben Breed was sliding into the front cockpit as I moved toward the rear one.

The ship was equipped with a self-starter. And the heat helped engine-starting along. She hummed twice, then caught. The prop spun, the engine roared. I reached down for helmet and goggles—the ship started to roll. She wasn't warm enough for the take-off—I groaned.

My eyes didn't pick up the plunge of the second bomb. But my ears picked up the roar it made when it struck earth. It was closer to the two-seater, ahead of us this time. The ship trembled as she rolled—a geyser of sand was flung up toward the hot sky.

Ben cut the switch, kicked right rudder, The two-seater rolled to a stop—then jerked forward as he advanced the throttle again. Fear struck at me—bombs were something you couldn't fight back. And a direct hit—

The plane was rolling to one side of the crater hole now. It wasn't such a big hole—but it was big enough. The drone of the ship above was drowned by the two-seater's engine. I tilted my head. The Wop's ship was diving, getting lower. He was trying hard for a hit.

"Get her—off!" I shouted hoarsely at Ben, but he didn't seem to hear me.

The two-seater was picking up speed—but we were rolling over rough ground now. And there was a slope ahead—we'd have to zoom over it.

"May be—out of bombs!" I muttered grimly. The wind was tearing at my leather helmet now.

And then the third one landed. The ship jerked sickeningly. The roar of the engine died. There was a sharp report as a tire burst. Sand and bits of mesquite battered down against the doped wing surfaces. The right wingtip slanted, crackled into the earth. A deep hole appeared to the right—a wheel of the two-seater dropped into it. The tail-assembly came up. Then, as the ship halted, it dropped back again.

Ben twisted his head, shouted. "Get over the side—run ten or fifteen feet—then drop flat! You're hit, see!"

I slid over the side, staggered away from the wrecked ship. I dropped to my knees, got up again. Five more feet—and I collapsed in a sprawl, rolled over on my back, flung my arms out.

The drone of the ship in the sky became a roar. Then it died abruptly. I opened my eyes slightly. The single-seater was diving down, directly over the plane. There was the clatter of machine-gun fire!

I groaned—then, as the Wop's stolen plane zoomed, I raised my head slightly. Ben Breed's body was hanging over the side of the fuselage, arms swinging down!

My head dropped back—I felt sort of smothered. Hit—or playing the game as he'd told me to play it? There was no way of telling—right away.

The Wop was banking his ship around—now he was diving again. Once more the prop-synchronized machine-gun spat lead down toward earth. A moving line of sand spurted up. I groaned, closed my eyes. The machine-gun lead was close to the plane—this time.

Then the ship was zooming again. At five hundred feet or so she came out of the zoom, went over in a bank. She circled above the slope. I closed my eyes, lay motionless. The drone became more distant. I stared up into the sky. The Wop was winging the little ship toward Mexico. He was flying almost directly south!

A minute or so passed. I sat up—stared into the sky. The ship was a tiny speck, far to the south. I got to my feet. Ben Breed's body was in the position it had been since the first burst of machine-gun fire. I ran toward the plane, calling out sharply.

"Ben—are you hit? Ben—"

His head came up suddenly. He twisted it, stared toward the south. There was a grim smile on his face. He shook his head slowly.

"Winged out, eh, Mac? Hurt—no lead in me! But it was close—"

I swore softly, "He thinks he got us, Ben—" I muttered. "You played it right—maybe it'll be a break for us."

Ben Breed nodded. But the expression on his face was a grim one.

"We'll *need* a break, Mac!" he muttered, "I had to play it this way—we piled into the hole made by that last bomb. But we can fix this ship up. We've got one chance—using a moll for the Wop. It's the only way to beat him—and his gang."

I reached for a pill. The little plane was lost in the hot glare of the sun.

"It's a tough spot for a girl," I muttered. "If you send her into—"

And then I got it. Something in his eyes—some slight expression of ironic amusement put me wise. I swore slowly and with feeling.

"*You?*" I muttered. "*You'll* play the moll?"

Ben Breed nodded. When he spoke, his voice held the same grim note it had held seconds ago.

"I'll play the moll, Mac—and I'll play her to the limit!" He reached for one of my pills. "It's the *one* way in—past the ghost guns!"

The Sky-Trap

*The duel to the finish between the
Federal men and the flying bandit.*

THE CLOUDS WERE piling up darkly to the northeast, and the wind was beginning to play tricks with the two-seater. I didn't like the looks of things, and told Ben so, through the phone-set strapped over our helmets.

"Want to hit Sojuan, Mac"—Ben called back to me from the front cockpit—"and get into the moll clothes."

I groaned. We were twenty minutes' flight from Sojuan, a tiny town about six miles across the Mex Line and east of Tia Juana. I wasn't strong for Ben Breed playing the moll stuff, anyway. It didn't seem to me he could get away with it But he was still the boss—and the way things had been going it looked as though this was our last chance at the Wop. Flores was fighting back hard, and that card trickster, Ganlin—*he* was sitting on the fence and trying to figure which way to jump. I had a hunch he'd side in with the Wop. Ben knew too much about Cards Ganlin.

The nose of the two-seater dropped suddenly; her left wing slanted downward. I could see Ben's head and shoulders move forward; he got the ship on even keel again. The roar of her engine, through the curved exhausts—that was steady enough. But the air was getting worse than bumpy. I spoke into the mouthpiece of the phone-set.

"Get down here—and make the moll change. We can pick up a pilot to hop the ship over closer to the lane, Ben!"

He twisted his head, and I caught a glimpse of a sardonic grin.

"You're guessing wrong, Mac," his voice came back. "We're winging—*across* the Line, this trip. And the worse weather we have—the easier it'll be."

I swore softly. My goggles were starting to mist from the spit of a rain that hadn't reached us in the regular form. Wind was bringing the spray on ahead. The nose of the ship slanted upward—we climbed. Ben Breed was roaring her up toward the clouds.

Relaxing in the seat, I felt my 'chute pack. It was my hunch that if the battered two-seater ever got tossed into a tail spin it would be a matter of going over the side. I wasn't strong for that little stunt.

The ship climbed, rocking from side to side and hitting air holes from time to time. I remembered a gent I'd once met in El Paso, and who had tried to tell me there were no such things as air holes. I wished he was riding along.

From the swaying of Ben Breed's head and shoulders I could guess how hard he was working over the stick and rudder bar of the crate. And I could guess how anxious he was to get into Tia Juana—and have a final crack at Antonio Flores. I swore again, wiped the glass of my goggles clear. Ben—playing his big card dolled up like a moll! Not so good.

The ship roared into the lower wisps of a gray-black cloud. She commenced to act funny—and then everything was a thick fog. Again and again I wiped my goggle glass clear. The roar of the engine was intensified in sound by the density of the atmosphere. It had a different sound. I could barely see the wing-tips of the crate—everything was soaked with water. For ten minutes she leaped and rolled through the wet—and Ben Breed worked. One thing was in our favor—we had a good wind blowing off the tail, and the crate picked up speed.

The nose of the ship dropped. The plane fell off on a wing, started to spin. The spin stopped in a hurry—but she dived through the gray-white stuff with the wires shrilling and the engine half throttled. And then, suddenly, we were out of it.

Everything was gray below. Sand and mesquite. But off to the right, toward the Pacific, were fairly high mountains. The Cocopahs, unless I was all wrong. And that meant that we were over Mexican soil, and quite a distance south of Tia Juana.

Twisting my head, I stared back past the tail assembly of the ship, downward. There was no sign of Tia Juana, but I did spot a road below, curving off toward the Pacific. Ben had twisted his head—he was nodding it.

"That's the Ensenada road—the curve westward to the coast We're—all right, Mac."

So far—we were. It looked as though we'd got across the Line in a ship, above the clouds, and had a good chance of getting down and making a decent landing. That meant that we had a chance of getting into Tia Juana without being spotted by any of the Wop's gang. And that was a lot. It was more than we'd been able to do in Juarez or in Ticardi.

But we weren't in yet. The ship was gliding with the engine throttled down to idling speed, and Ben Breed was handling her sweetly. We dropped about five thousand feet, and I started to look around for a landing spot. The crate wasn't so fast that she needed a lot of room, but she needed considerable earth, and it had to be fairly level.

Five hundred feet off the mesquite-covered sandy soil Ben gave her the gun. She roared along, losing altitude in a shallow glide, and headed back toward Tia Juana. Lower and lower she dropped. I was sitting stiffly in the rear cockpit. We got down to within a hundred yards of the earth, then fifty. But the ship roared on, northward. I commenced to get shaky about it.

"If they have some of the boys outside of town—" I muttered through the phone-set—"we'll be spotted."

Ben caught part of what I said. He nodded his head.

"Half right, Mac," he shot back. "A *ship'll* be spotted, coming from the south."

Then the roar of the two-seater's engine died abruptly; the nose of the plane dropped. I stared over the leading edge of the right wing's lower surface, got a glimpse of a level stretch, dotted with clumps of blue-gray mesquite. The ship dropped, struck sand. Her wheels ripped through a mesquite clump— her tail assembly came up. I swore harshly—and then the tail assembly was dropping back again. Ben had the stick held back against his stomach.

The plane rolled perhaps fifty yards, came to a halt. Wind raised up the sand in eddies; Ben Breed jerked his head, ripping the phone apparatus, helmet and goggles, from it. He grinned.

"We'll hop out—and stake her down. Toss out the bag with the moll clothes in it. Let's work fast."

I got rid of my own helmet and goggles, snapped the safety belt buckle loose, and slipped down to the earth, first tossing the brown bag down. In ten minutes we had the crate staked down, with rope on her wing-tips and over the tail assembly. There was no sign of any habitation—the country was not irrigated in the section. It was dry, semi-desert land. Cacti and sand—and mesquite. I lighted a pill, and stared northward. Ben Breed came to my side, grinned.

"Not that way, Mac," he stated. "Tia's over there."

He pointed to the northwest. I frowned at him.

"How far?" I asked grimly.

Ben grunted. "Maybe eight miles—with a rise of land between the town and this spot. The road's about four miles west of here, and that's the way we'll head."

"Ben"—I started slowly—"I'm just as anxious to grab off, or to knock off, the Wop—as you are. It means that I'll be squared up with the bank back in Arizona. It means a nice wad of reward money. And it means a bad *hombre* out of the way. But get this—he won't fall for this woman stuff."

Ben smiled grimly. His lean face was over the brown bag now. A fine mist of rain was in the air. It was getting chilly. Ben straightened. His gray eyes met mine. He spoke in his husky voice.

"Mac," he stated, "you and me—we've chased Flores up and down the Border plenty. He's done nothing but damage, all the way. He's set to do more. We can't depend on Ganlin—not now. And the Wop's out to rub us off the map. This is our last crack at him. He's wise to most disguise stuff—he's known when we were coming in close to him, in the past. He *doesn't* know, this time. And I'm not playing a looker, Mac."

I stared at him.

"You can't get to the Wop any other way," I stated. "He likes the sweet—"

'There was a moll in El Paso'—Ben cut in grimly—"and Flores got sick of her. He tried to ship her south, and it didn't take. The police picked her up—and she put up bail, then ducked. The Wop would like to know where she is. He'd like to know so that he could make certain she'd stay in one place—and be finished talking. The frail's name was Doll Bernoni. At least, that was one of them. I'm a friend of hers, when I get into the rags."

I stared at Ben. He was smiling slightly. Reaching into the bag, he pulled out a black wig.

"Her name *was* Bernoni?" I muttered.

"Correct," Ben stated, and jerked the wig over his hair. "She stepped between two half-breeds who were shooting it out in a Juarez drink shack—and became a 'was.'"

I didn't say a thing. Ben commenced to get into a lot of rags that were colorless, and sort of bulky. He got them on right over his own clothes. And he didn't make any fuss about it. When he got finished he looked like Ben Breed—dolled up as a Mex woman. It wasn't much of a disguise. I told him so, and he seemed to agree with me.

"Mac," he said slowly, "I'm going in after the Wop. I'm not going to get close enough to him to worry about my face." He reached down and pulled a veil out of the brown bag. It was long, black. He wound it about his head. "I'm in mourning, Mac," he stated grimly, "for Antonio Flores."

I swore softly. "It isn't that easy, Ben," I stated, "and you know it. What's the game?"

He spoke in a low tone. The wind kicked up gusts of sand, rustled the mesquite clumps and shrilled gently through the wires of the two-seater. I stood motionlessly, and listened. After a few minutes Ben finished talking. His eyes were narrowed. He inspected two weapons—one had a Maxim silencer attached—the other didn't. There was a little silence. Then Ben spoke.

"Well?" His voice held an ironic, amused note. "It's a good one, isn't it, Mac? If it works!"

I smiled grimly. "It's damned good!" I replied slowly. "But if it doesn't work—"

Ben Breed swore. He slipped one gun inside a pocket in the drab skirt. The other he stared down upon, smiling slightly.

"We're dealing the cards so that it *does* work, Mac," he stated slowly. "It'll take a high hand to beat the deal."

I nodded. "The Wop knows how to draw 'em," I reminded. "He's held high hands before—and he plays them cool-like."

"The game's almost over, Mac." Ben spoke in his husky voice. "The Wop's been slipping them into his hand from beneath the table. It's a gambler's chance—this one. We're taking it."

I nodded again. "Sky trap!" I breathed slowly. "And if it don't work—"

I paused, looked into Ben's eyes. He was smiling coldly.

"—we won't be around—to worry about it, Mac," he stated grimly. "Let's go!"

I SAT ON the chair, and my back was close to the white-washed wall at the far end of the room. It was an hour since Ben and I had reached the south end of Tia Juana, and Ben had gone on ahead. I had come along slowly, keeping on the main road, and had reached the Yellow House without running into anyone who looked suspicious, or who might think *I* looked that way. At least, that was the way I figured.

My right hand was in the pocket of my khaki jacket, and it gripped metal. I was expecting a visitor, and anxious to see the gent. It meant that Ben was crashing through with his plan—if my visitor arrived. And if he didn't arrive—

I didn't like to think about that. It was almost four o'clock, and outside the hotel known as the Yellow House it was raining a bit, and blowing a bit more. Dirt was becoming mud. The horses weren't running at the track along the Border line, a half-mile from town. It was out of season for racing—but not for gambling and drinking. Tia Juana was the same as ever, in that respect.

The room I sat in was located in the rear of the Yellow House. There was no upper floor. I could hear the raid patter on the roof. There was the feeling that we were trapped—and I swore rather frequently because the feeling existed. Sitting waiting— that had a lot to do with it.

The knob of the door moved. So did the cloth of my coat pocket. I hadn't heard any footfalls, and there was a hall outside of the room. It wasn't carpeted, and the boards had creaked when I'd come down it. My eyes narrowed on the knob—it moved back to where it had started from.

There was one window in the room—just one. It hadn't any shade, and it opened on a narrow alley. The window was on my right as I faced the door. I looked toward it. There was no particular reason why the knob should have moved back again—the door wasn't locked.

Something moved—beyond the window. My heart stopped

jumping around, and I got sort of cold. That made two of them—one at the door, the other at the window. My body tense, I waited.

The knob turned again—I got that movement in a glance. There was dark color beyond the window—a sort of blurred shadow. A shadow without sun. The door opened. No one stood beyond it. I called out:

"Come on in, Cards!"

My voice was a bit shaky—I was trying to watch the window and the door at the same time. And I was trying to be cheerful.

A figure came into sight. It came through the door, head low, hunched forward. I came close to squeezing lead. The figure came through like a football player hitting the line. Only the arms and hands were dangling. There was a crash—the figure sprawled on the faded yellow carpet of the room. I sucked in my breath sharply.

I didn't move. My eyes went to the window in a flickering glance. The shadow outside had vanished. I stared down at the man sprawled perhaps six feet from me. The carpet near the man's right side wasn't so yellow now. It was turning a darker shade. I kept my gun leveled on the door, inside my right pocket. One thing was certain—the man lying on the carpet in the room hadn't *walked* down the hall. He'd been carried, and carried quietly.

Seconds passed. The stain on the carpet spread. I slid out of the chair, got over against the left wall, moved toward the door. I glanced toward the window—something glittered.

I dropped—and at the same second a gun pop-coughed outside the window. The glass didn't splinter—but the plaster above my head cracked. I fell heavily—and stayed down. Nothing else happened.

A few more seconds passed. I turned my head and stared at the hole in the window glass. Then I crawled toward the figure that hadn't moved since it had pitched into the room. I got fingers on a wrist. The man was dead. I worked my way toward the window, stood up slowly, opened it. There was no sign of any one in the alley.

I moved back and stared down at the figure lying face downward on the carpet. I listened. The Yellow House desk—such as it was—was down the hall about twenty-five yards. The hotel was old and poorly built. I'd taken a pretty heavy fall—and so had the man at my feet. Yet no one came. It wasn't so good.

Leaning down, I rolled the man over on his back. I stiffened, swore grimly. Bullets had ripped over, under and into the dead man's heart. And the dead man was the one I'd been expecting. He was the one Ben Breed had been hunting. He was Cards Ganlin!

THE ALLEY WAS wet and deserted. I slid out of the window, kept close to the wood and 'dobe side of the Yellow House. I moved toward the *Avenida,* not far distant. My eyes were narrowed, but I wasn't missing much. The first part of the game had failed. Ironically. I wanted to spot Ben Breed—in a woman's shabby dress and a mourning veil. The symbolism of the veil and color—it wasn't pleasant.

Ben had left me to find Cards Ganlin. He was going to learn the truth from Cards. He wanted to know which way he was tossing the cards. If the answer was favorable, Cards was to be sent to me. A little fear was gripping me now. Cards *had* been sent on—but he'd been bullet-crashed out, first. The Wop was in on the deal—but where was Ben Breed? How had the men who had carried Cards silently down the hall of the Yellow House and pitched him into the room known where I was?

There was just one chance—they had learned where Cards was going from *that* gent, and not from Ben. Granting that, why had Cards been delivered? The Wop was done with warnings. He'd been pressed too closely.

I twisted my neck. No one was trailing. No one, so far as I could see. I was nearing the *Avenida*. The rain was letting up a bit, but it had made plenty of mud. The wind was blowing in gusts.

There weren't many humans walking Tia Juana's main stem. The gambling houses were doing a good business. I turned to the left, headed toward the Foreign Club. It was the safest place in Tia, when there was a jam on. Ben might be there— he might not. But I was reasonably sure that the Wop would not be there. The Federal authorities wanted him—and he was known to them. More arrests had been made in the Foreign Club than in any other single spot in Tia Juana.

I slowed down. My eyes had gone across the paving of the *Avenida*. Something that looked like a woman was crossing toward me. There was a shabby, flowing skirt, a shawl—a black veil. The figure moved slowly—very slowly. It moved with a slight limp. The head was bent low, and the shawl was wrapped tightly around it, covering most of the face.

I moved along near the curb, and the figure crossed back of me. I was walking slowly. A voice sounded—very low.

"Did Cards—come?"

I nodded my head. Ben Breed walked at my side, not looking at me. His head was bent low.

"He was—delivered," I breathed softly. "Dead."

Out of the corners of my eyes I saw Ben's body jerk. He moved a little ahead of me now—spoke again.

"Job on—in town. Wop's in—and the gang's tagging his heels. Head for the bar of the Foreign Club. I'll be in—"

Ben halted, leaned forward. I saw a coin glittering on the muddy paving. He picked it up. I walked on toward the Foreign Club, without looking back. Ben had taken a jolt—he hadn't even suspected that Cards was to be rubbed out.

I reached the parking grounds, walked through them, went into the Club. There was quite a crowd inside; most of the Mexicans were playing the card games—a mixed crowd of Americans were working the wheels. The bar was in the rear of the place—I moved toward it, ordered a golden fizz. It felt good going down, and better after it arrived. I tried a second, and drank to Ganlin's passing out.

Then I turned my back to the bar; and waited for a shabbily dressed woman to enter. Five minutes passed; there was no sign of Ben. I commenced to get nervous. I had a beer, and as I was draining the glass there was a sharp *crack*—outside the Club. The bartender was wiping up the wood in front of me, and I must have showed the way I felt. He grinned.

"Car exhaust, Mac!" he stated, and though he'd used my right name unconsciously it gave me another jump. "We don't bump 'em off that way—around here."

I tried to grin. Putting the glass on the bar, I faced the room again. The humans playing at the gaming tables hadn't paid any attention to the shotlike sound.

Then I stiffened. Ben Breed was coming in through the main entrance. He was walking with a grin on his face, and he was dressed in his own clothes—the ones he had been wearing beneath the moll rags. He walked pretty straight—more so than usual. Coming down through the rows of gambling tables, he reached my side.

"Hello, Mac!" he greeted. "How's tricks?" He stared at the bartender. "Scotch—straight," he ordered. "Ben Breed's celebrating."

I stood motionlessly, my eyes narrowed on Ben's. There was a broad grin on his face. The bartender shoved across the Scotch—Ben tossed down a bill. As the bartender moved toward the cash register, Ben slid the glass toward him, tilted it sharply. The liquor struck the gutter outside of the bar. Some of it splashed on me. Ben lifted the glass—he was taking it away from his lips as the bartender tossed his change on the wood.

"What's the celebration, Ben?" I muttered grimly.

The bartender was doing something back of the wood, but it seemed to me he was listening to us pretty carefully. Ben laughed harshly.

"The Wop's gone down," he stated grimly. "He ate a half dozen pieces of warm lead."

I stiffened. The bartender swore.

Ben grinned at me. "It's all up, Mac," he stated. "A half-breed named Malino got him. Let's head back for San Diego—fly out before it gets dark. The sky won't be so bad—the rain's letting up."

I blinked. Ben gripped me by an arm. He was grinning.

"Rotten way for the Wop to go out, eh? Sitting in a cheap back room—and getting the dose without even fingering his own gat. The Mex cops are down there now—let's get going, Mac. It'll be dark in an hour or so—"

He broke off, pulled me away from the bar. He chuckled. I

walked along by his side; The last thing I'd seen, before turning away, was the bartender's face. It was grim, set in a funny half-smile. But the eyes held a cruel expression.

We went down through the tables, and got outside the Foreign Club. We turned southward, toward the road that ran to Ensenada. The wind was blowing in cold gusts. I stared at Ben.

"What in hell's the game?" I snapped in a low voice. "The Wop's not—"

"— dead?" Ben's voice was cold. "Check, Mac. He's fighting like hell—that gent is! Got a man in the Foreign Club—spotting us."

I blinked. Then I got it.

"The bartender?" I muttered. "That fellow?"

"Check again!" Ben replied. "That's 'Mushy' Freen—and the bulls just ran him out of Seattle a few days ago. He's come down fast—and headed right for the Wop's camp. Flores figured he could use him."

We were moving along the road now. I looked back toward the town. The Foreign Club was almost on the southern outskirts. There was no one following us.

"You walked in—playing it straight!" I muttered. "You took one sweet chance—I heard a shot, and it sounded—"

"Exhaust back-fire," Ben cut in. "Gave me a jump, though. And the idea. You see—I spotted Freen before I met you. He was outside of the Club, in the back, smoking a pill. I was looking things over. He's yellow—and he's never killed a man."

I was thinking back. "How about Cards?" I muttered. "They got him—and they damn near got me, back in that room."

Ben nodded. "No trouble finding Cards," he stated grimly.

"I grabbed him in the Green Fan. He was drinking—alone. Asked him how he was playing it. He didn't look very happy. I got the idea that the Wop was out after him, and that he knew it. He wanted to know where the money was. I told him there was five grand waiting for him over in your room. He went out the back way. I followed."

We were cutting off from the road now. The going was rougher. Ben Breed stopped, looked back. No one was in sight.

"Cards got about two hundred yards down the alley back of the Green Fan—and then he got rubbed out. Knife in the back—and a lot of lead as he swung around. But he squirmed, Mac—he squirmed at the finish."

Ben's voice was hoarse. He was moving over the sand and mesquite, wet with the rain, with a steady stride.

"He got rid of my name—and gave the room number and the Yellow House name. From where I was hiding out I heard that much—I wasn't fifty yards back of him, and he was crying out—at the finish. Someone figured they'd get me, maybe—"

I nodded my head. That wasn't hard to figure. Shove the dead body of Ganlin into the room—and when there was movement, let loose lead through the alley window. It had come close to working, at that. But not on Breed.

"What's our play?" I muttered. "Are we running out?"

Ben swore sharply. He spoke in a cold tone.

"Sky trap, Mac—only in a different way. We can't use Cards now—they licked us on that deal."

We moved along for perhaps a quarter of a mile, in silence. Then Ben Breed slipped a hand into a pocket of the jacket he was wearing. He spoke in a low tone.

"After the kill, Mac—I headed back toward the Green Fan.

Got about fifty feet along the alley—when there was a shot. Then a crash—and a human pitched down off the roof of a shack just ahead of me. I got a glimpse of a second human, slipping off the roof, but he hadn't fired the shot. Ducked back of some kegs—and watched the crowd pile in. There was a lot of excitement. I was fairly safe—went out and hobbled along the alley, picking up scraps. Got close to the crowd—heard a Mex use Flores' name. Gave me a jolt—thought he'd gone out. Got a look at the face of the dead man. He was dead, all right—and he looked a lot like the Wop. But he *wasn't* the Wop, Mac!"

I swore. Ben Breed was smiling. He halted suddenly, turned. His eyes went up toward the sky over Tia Juana. Then he turned, and we moved along again.

"See the game? Flores was playing a pal as a double—and sitting back, waiting for us to come in. And for Cards to come in. The double was the bait."

I grunted. "Who got the double?" I asked grimly. "The other fellow on the roof?"

Ben shook his head. "The other fellow—that was Flores," he said slowly. "He was waiting for me to get in close. The double went out from a rifle bullet—it was a sweet shot. On the *Avenida,* while I was looking for any one worth seeing, I spotted 'Sharpshooter' Burke. He's always hung around Cards. Ten to one it was his lead that got the Wop's double."

We walked on. "You were dolled up in woman-clothes," I stated. "How come the Wop spotted you—was waiting for you?"

Ben smiled grimly. "I had to talk to Cards," he reminded. "They had him spotted. There was just one play for me—and

I took it. The last card, Mac. I got out of the rags—and used you for conversation. Mushy was the target. He'll run out—to see if the Wop's dead. He'll learn he isn't. Ten to one he'll feed Flores the news that I think he's out of the play. And the Wop is clever. He'll think I think the same way. Didn't I get a flash of the double he was using?"

I nodded. "And you spread the news that we were heading for the crate—to fly out before dark!" I muttered. "Freen will hand out that info, sure thing."

Ben nodded. "It's the last chance, Mac," he stated. "It's my hunch that the Wop'll come in person this time."

"To the ship?" I muttered. "Alone?"

Ben Breed shook his head. "Not so likely," he muttered. "And *how* he'll come—that's not sure. The crate's the bait, Mac—we'll hide out—and wait."

I groaned. "It may be mob stuff," I stated slowly. "We can't handle the gang."

Ben shook his head slowly. He halted, looked back of him. There was no sign of any human. Then he looked toward the sky, and I got the idea.

"He'll wing over!" I muttered. "You know what that means, Ben—he's got the best ship—and a chance to—"

Ben swore harshly. "There was a job on in Tia," he muttered. "It isn't on—not now. We're more important, Mac—and the Wop's in a fighting mood. He got Cards Ganlin—and he lost his double. It's a sky trap—but he doesn't know it. His brain won't work that way. I figure he's finished, see. I'm careless—winging out. I'm tickled. That's his way of figuring. He'll come hunting for this ship of ours—or trailing us. He may not come alone, but he won't bring the mob. They'll handle the job—and the Tia Juana police can play with them. We want the Wop—we're playing the final hand."

We moved onward. Sky trap? We'd tried traps before. The Wop was still in the clear. He was still fighting. He had a faster ship—and he could handle it. I muttered to myself as we moved over the soaked sand and mesquite. The air would be rough—

Ben Breed chuckled harshly. He was moving with his body hunched forward, his face set grimly. He spoke hoarsely.

"It's been a scrap—all the way, Mac. You've stuck fine. A lot of boys have gone out—some of 'em were good boys. Most were bad. With the Wop out of the way—some of the others will talk. And without Flores they'll be rounded up. He's the brains—the fighter of the outfit. He's given me the toughest man-hunt I've had, Mac. This time—it's one of us out, and the other up."

I nodded my head slightly. Fear struck at me momentarily. Ben Breed was staking everything on the final draw. The Wop had been a pretty consistent winner. If he came now—in the fast plane—

A gust of wind caught us as we topped a rise in the sand. Ben lowered his head against it. His hands were out of his pockets now. His face held a mask-like expression. His fists were clenched, swinging at his sides. One thing was sure—Breed was set for a fight. He was playing against Antonio Flores—to the finish.

BOTH OF US were lying flat on the sand beside the two-seater, when we saw the two figures coming toward the plane. They were coming slowly, creeping over the sand, through the mesquite, from two different directions.

"If it's the mob—" I muttered hoarsely—"we'd better get into the air—"

I broke off. Ben was getting his Colt ready for action. He kept raising his head slightly, and staring up toward the sky. I groaned. If the Wop were to wing over, and those on the ground were to close in—

"A hell of a sky trap!" I muttered. "If we don't get off in a hurry—"

Ben Breed swore sharply. A shot sounded—the sand leaped in a little spurt, several feet beyond a wing-tip of the plane.

"Playing it safe, he muttered. "Can't spot us—but they *can* spot the ship. Trying to get an engine or gas tank hit."

I nodded. Ten miles across the Line, in Mexico. The ship down—and the Wop's gang closing in on us. It didn't look good.

Ben twisted his head toward mine. Another shot sounded. This time I saw sand kick up in a spurt, nearer the plane.

"Got to—get off!" Ben muttered. "Can't risk—a hit. Didn't figure they'd play that way. Wop's orders."

I smiled grimly. The Wop was clever. He was playing for the plane first—they could get us after.

Ben was getting to his feet. He spoke sharply, as I got to mine. We both kept the plane between us and the crawling men, and bent low.

"You get the tail-assembly loose from the stake—I'll handle the wing-tip stakes. They're still short—in range!"

I nodded, moved toward the tail assembly. Two more shots sounded. Sand spurted, back of the ship. I was pulling up the stake now, slipping the rope over the tail portion of the fuselage. I heard the crack of Ben's gun.

Then I was moving toward the rear cockpit. There was no gun mounted in it—but Ben had mounted and synchronized a Browning on the front cockpit cowling. And Ben could shoot. If we got the two-seater off, there would be a chance. But the sky trap had failed. We hadn't pulled the Wop in carelessly.

Ben was climbing into the front cockpit now. He had got the wing-tip fastenings loose—and was bending low in the fuse-lage. Shots sounded—perhaps a half dozen of them—but they were all short in range. The self-starter clattered—the engine roared, then died abruptly.

Fear gripped me. If the engine failed now—

The self-starter clattered again. We had warmed the engine up, less than fifteen minutes ago—there was not likely to be anything wrong with it. I twisted my head as it roared again, then spluttered. A figure was rising, less than fifty yards back of the ship. I swung around—raised my automatic, squeezed the trigger. Something cracked sharply into a strut of the ship—wood splintered. I swore fiercely. The man had a rifle—and my chance of a hit at the distance had been very slight.

The ship was rolling forward now. The roar of the engine was steadier. But the rain had soaked into the sand—the earth was sluggish. The exhaust beat drowned the crackle of rifle and automatic fire—I dropped down into the cockpit.

Figures were rising as I twisted my head. I counted four men—two had rifles, the others were armed with small guns. I muttered a little prayer that Ben would get the two-seater off without doing a ground loop. There were too many for us—a crash and we were finished.

Then the wheels and tail-skid of the ship was lifting off the sand. A rise loomed ahead—the nose of the ship came up. We zoomed. The beat of the engine was steady now. Ben banked the ship steeply—she came around. Then he leveled her off, climbed her again.

My eyes were stinging—I jerked the goggles down over my helmet. Ben had his over his eyes—but there had been no time to adjust the phone-set apparatus. I stared over the side of the fuselage as the two-seater ship climbed.

Below, in a circle, I counted five men. It had been a close go. Once more we had failed in an attempt to trap Antonio Flores. Once again we had barely escaped a hail of bullets. Several of the men were on their feet now—red flashed from a rifle one of them held.

I smiled grimly. Not much chance of a hit from the earth. My eyes went to the sand below again, as the plane banked sharply. The air was rough—very rough. The two-seater was twisted by the gusts of wind sweeping the dark clouds overhead. By the roar of the engine I could guess that Ben Breed had the throttle advanced all the way.

The man my eyes were watching suddenly slumped to the ground. I swore sharply. My eyes went to another man, not far from the one who had gone down. Treachery—fighting among the gang members?

And then I saw—the others! They were coming in toward the spot from which we had taken off, in a semi-circle. There were perhaps a dozen of them—and they wore khaki-colored uniforms. Mexican police. Surrounding the Wop's men!

Ben saw them, too. He got an arm out in the prop wash, pointed down as the ship banked around. He shouted hoarsely.

"Mex—they're caught!"

I nodded. But I was thinking of the Wop. Was he down there,

trapped with the others? Were the Mexican police closing in on him, too?

The plane fell off on a wing—and I caught my breath sharply. We were too close to the earth for a slip. Wind battered at the side of my face—the nose of the two-seater dropped—then came up again. The ship zoomed, came out of the zoom into a climb. I breathed deeply.

Ben Breed jerked his head. His face held a grim smile. He shouted above the beat of the engine.

"Coming—from the west—Mac! *The Wop!*"

I twisted my head, followed the direction in which Ben had turned his head. From an air spot west of Tia Juana, back of the hills on that side of the town, a ship was rushing through the air. A small ship. Flores' ship!

Ben was banking the two-seater away from the smaller plane, and heading straight toward the Border line. The little ship had perhaps two hundred more feet of altitude than we had—and she was coming in from an angle, edging against the stiff wind.

The fight on the ground was behind us, now. We were less than a half mile north of the spot—and bucking the stiff wind. The two-seater was acting pretty badly in the gusts.

I reached into my pocket and got my automatic loose. It didn't seem so funny—even though my chances of getting a hit *were* small. The Wop had altitude—and a fast ship. We had a slow plane, hard to maneuver—and were winging closer to earth than Flores.

My lips moved—I muttered a few words to myself. The chips were being shoved out now. This was the last play of the game. There was no chance for Ben or myself to squirm into the 'chute packs—and there wasn't enough altitude to use them—had we been able to get inside of the harness.

Three hundred feet above the sand and mesquite—we were. The Wop's ship was about five hundred. Ben had ceased to climb the two-seater—he was roaring her straight toward the Border line now. And we weren't far from it.

I smiled grimly. Ben was playing for high stakes—to the finish. He was sacrificing climb, his chance to get equal altitude with the Wop—and trying to get near enough to the U.S.A. so that if he *did* shoot Flores down we'd have our man. He was trying—but the single-seater was very close to us now—and coming in from the left. I twisted my head—caught sight of the barrel of the cowl-mounted gun.

The little ship was piquing on us now. Her nose was coming down. Our nose dropped, as Ben jerked his head, then turned it to the front again. Then the nose came up—we'd got speed in a dive—now we were zooming.

Above the beat of the engine there sounded the staccato clatter of machine-gun fire. I ducked my head, instinctively. The two-seater was banking vertically, coming around. The Wop had missed with the first burst from his machine-gun.

My head came up. A shape flashed across the nose of our plane. I heard Ben let loose a burst from his gun. Then we were diving straight toward the sand below—and the shape was zooming. I groaned.

We came out of the dive, went into an almost vertical zoom. The roar of the engine became a drone, a high-pitched pull-song. The nose came down—we banked as the engine resumed its natural beat again. Once more there sounded the staccato clatter of machine-gun bullets. I twisted my head. We hadn't got *enough* altitude in the zoom. The Wop had his ship back of us—above us.

"Dive her!" I screamed hoarsely, and swung around in the small cockpit.

The nose of the ship went down. I could see red streaming out from the muzzle of the Wop's machine-gun. Wing fabric ripped—on my right. I raised my automatic, and the rush of wind battered it to one side.

Then the two-seater was zooming. Her nose pointed straight up at the clouds. I saw the Wop's ship zoom, too. She came up with more speed than the heavier, slower plane. It looked hopeless. The Wop could fly—and more than that, he had a ship under him!

We were over on our back now—I sucked in my breath sharply. The shape that had been back of us, getting altitude—was directly in front of us! A crackling beat sounded from the front cockpit. A strut leaped—close to my head. And then the little ship was off on a wing—she was plunging toward the earth, red trailing back from her engine!

Ben Breed had scored a hit! He had shot the Wop's ship down out of the sky—as the two-seater was over in a loop, on her back!

We were plunging downward now— the earth stabbed up at us. I cried out, fiercely—it didn't seem possible that Ben could pull us up in time to save a crash. But he did!

The landing-gear skimmed over a slope of mesquite—the nose came up. Above the roar of the engine there sounded a grinding, tearing crash. Ahead of us was a great cloud of black smoke—red flame streaked upward and along the earth.

The roar of our ship engine died abruptly. Ben Breed was staring over the side—the earth was less than ten feet below the ship. Something white flashed back—a marker. A Border marker.

And then the landing gear—wheels and tail-skid—struck the sand. It was a fast landing—we bounced once. Ben pulled back on the stick—the two-seater lost flying speed. We struck for the second time. The ship rolled forward. Her speed was very slow—when she nosed into mesquite that was too thick. The tail-assembly came up—the propeller dug in, splintered.

I threw my arms before my face—but there wasn't much of a jolt. Both of us slid out of our cockpits—ran toward the flaming wreckage of the single-seater. She was scattered over a lot of ground—but it was U.S.A. ground.

We both had our weapons out, ready for action. No taking chances with Antonio Flores. Ben pointed off toward the wreckage of the fuselage. It was perhaps fifty yards from the wings of the ship. We ran toward it.

The Wop was lying with his arms at his side, half out of the fuselage. His face was ghastly, but he was conscious. Ben Breed moved up close to him, but he didn't attempt to get him out of the wreckage. Flores' eyes told the story—he was finished.

But he smiled. Red streaked his lips. They moved. He uttered four words—broken, hoarse. The scar on his face gleamed as he spoke.

"Border—Brand—too—late!"

Then he closed his eyes. I turned away. The Wop was a killer. A crook. A double-crosser. He was a lot of other things. But he had been game. And now he was dead.

I walked a few feet away, dropped down in the wet sand. I lighted a pill. My fingers were shaking pretty badly. After a while Ben Breed came over my way. His long arms hung at his sides; his face was sober. His gray eyes met mine; he spoke in his husky voice.

"We win, Mac—the gang's licked. They'll talk plenty, with the Wop out of things. You'll be in the clear with that bank of yours. There's reward coin—a lot of it. And things'll quiet down some—along the Border."

I nodded. Ben dropped down beside me. He rolled one of his black-papered pills. I was thinking of the Wop's last words. A sort of tribute—the first two—for Ben? I decided to figure them that way. My lips moved.

"It was a tough fight Ben," I said slowly. "It took doing!"

Ben Breed smiled with his gray eyes. It seemed to me that he looked a bit younger. Imagination, of course, but I let that go, too. Ben pulled on the black paper of the cigarette.

"It took a *lot* of doing, Mac—" he stated slowly, huskily—"and most of it was—Border Brand!"

About the Author

RAOUL WHITFIELD WAS one
of the group of our earliest acquain-
tances. He was a hard, patient,
determined worker. His style from
the first was hard and brittle and
over-inclined to staccato. Later, he
became more fluent and went along,
shoulder to shoulder, with the best of
them. Earlier, a newspaperman, he wrote
from knowledge of men, and women, and their ways.

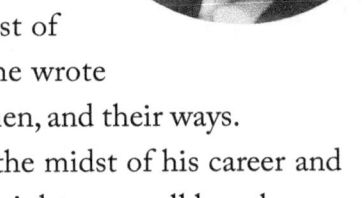

Personal tragedy intervened in the midst of his career and
death, this past year, cut off what might very well have been a
brilliant future.

Whit was ambitious. He wanted to invade other fields than
that of crime detection and criminal conflict.

Long and fascinating were the discussions between Whit
and Dash. Whit maintained that, given characters and a
general plot, it was a cinch to write a detective story. When in
a spot, all you need do, is to use the well-known props. A good
writer should produce a novel without any of these appurte-
nances to achieve effect. And Dash's comeback, "All right, if
you want to make it the hard way, try writing a book omitting
every word that has the letter 'f' for example."

—Joseph T. Shaw

www.ingramcontent.com/pod-product-compliance
Lightning Source LLC
Chambersburg PA
CBHW072355030726
47505CB00014B/1847